Riding on Duke's Train

Riding on Duke's Train

Mick Carlon

A LeapKids Book
Leapfrog Kids
Leapfrog Press
Teaticket, Massachusetts

A LeapKids Book
Leapfrog Kids

Published in 2012 in the United States by
Leapfrog Press LLC
PO Box 2110
Teaticket, MA 02536
www.leapfrogpress.com

Printed in the United States of America

Distributed in the United States by
Consortium Book Sales and Distribution
St. Paul, Minnesota 55114
www.cbsd.com

First Edition

ISBN: 978-1-935248-06-4

Library of Congress Cataloging-in-Publication Data

TK

Manufactured by Thomson-Shore, Dexter, MI (USA); RMA577RC918, November, 2011

To my parents, George and Peggy Carlon

For the itinerary of the 1939 European tour, the author is indebted to John Edward Hasse's superb biography *Beyond Category: The Life and Genius of Duke Ellington* (Da Capo Press, 1993).

List of References

One

So there I was in old Paris, gazing over the gypsy's glowing crystal ball with Rex.

"What do you see, Madame?" Rex asked her, shooting me a wink.

The wrinkly woman looked up. "Do you like hamburgers?" she asked.

Rex chuckled. "Well, sure—who doesn't?"

Two bloodshot eyes lingered first on me, then on Rex. I could feel the tingles zig-zagging up my spine.

"Don't," she said. "That will be ten francs."

"Can you believe that old crow?" chuckled Rex, as we stepped back onto the rue de l'Harpe. I easily kept up with my chubby yet fleet friend.

"Man, she had eyes like an angry old muskrat's," I said.

It was April, 1939, and Rex and I—along with the

rest of the Duke Ellington Orchestra—had been in Paris a week. For me, an eleven-year-old boy from the back woods of Georgia, the trip had been one wonder after another.

"Your belly's not *that* big, Rex," I said, trying to find *some* explanation for the old gypsy's words.

Checking out his round reflection in a bakery window, Rex frowned. "Cootie's got a bigger gut than me—and Sonny out-eats us both. Anyways, I'm hungry—let's find a café."

The afternoon was cool and breezy, with plump blimpy clouds floating over the city. Finding a café on the Boulevard St. Michel, we were soon both diving into bowls of onion soup and frothy mugs of *café au lait.*

"Beats chitlins, doesn't it?" I asked.

"Actually, Daniel, I'm partial to Southern cooking," said Rex, who talked like a professor, read four or five books at once, and was constantly jotting down his impressions of the world in a calf-skin journal. (Not to mention playing one of the most supple, lyrical cornets in all of jazz). A few stray crumbs fell onto his shirt. "Remember, both Duke and I hail from Washington, which is decidedly a Southern town."

"Did you know him when you were my age?" I asked.

Two lovely French gals smiled at Rex as they sauntered by. Tipping his hat, he smiled back—an action that could get a black man lynched back home in Georgia. I was liking Paris more all the time.

"Remember, lad, I'm eight years younger than the Gov'nor—with a few less bags beneath my eyes. But one broiling summer day when I was a wee lad, I dove into the deep end of the YMCA pool—where I had no business being, seeing that I couldn't swim. Man, everybody was having so much fun that they didn't notice little old me going down for the last time. But then Duke—his pals called him that even back then—dove in and yanked me up to the fresh air. Now, he swears he doesn't recall that day—but I sure do! And that was my introduction to Edward Kennedy Ellington. Hey, speaking of the man, we have a rehearsal in about thirty minutes. Let's scarf down this chow, Daniel, and scram."

Two

I figure now's a fine time to tell you about *my* introduction to Edward Kennedy Ellington. I don't quite believe the details of this tale myself, so if you're a bit disbelieving, I can't say that I blame you.

Now please don't bother feeling all weepy for me (because I have no memory of it), but when I was ten months old my folks died in a car wreck in Tennessee. I was asleep in the back seat and stayed in the car, but my mom and pop were thrown through the windshield and died. The drunken white man who plowed his truck into our Tin Lizzy never spent a day in jail either.

My pop's mom grabbed a train to rescue me from the orphanage. Turned out that old Pop had purchased a healthy life insurance policy so Granny and I lived snug and comfortable in her rented cottage in the woods outside of Helen, Georgia.

Riding on Duke's Train

One afternoon in late May of 1937, I walked home from school to find old Granny dead in her rocker on the front porch. Her eyes were wide open and she was smiling, so I figured her end hadn't been too tough to take. Naturally, I was sad—but old Granny had been reminding me that this day was coming for years, so I wasn't too surprised.

After burying her in the woods behind the cottage, I grabbed a gunny sack and threw in some clothes and all the cash money Granny kept in her strong box beneath her bed. Then, after locking up our old cottage good and tight, I hit the road.

A Georgia dusk in May can snatch your breath away, with the sky as red as the clay beneath your feet. I walked for hours, not seeing a soul, hearing only the insects and the owls. A crater-filled moon lit my way.

Are you up there, Granny? I thought to myself—but if she was, she wasn't letting on.

Near midnight I came to a clearing—and rightly gasped. For before me stood a sleek silver train—a silver engine pulling four silver cars, each one soaking up and shooting out all that moonlight.

"Shoo, now! Get going!" yelled the conductor to a mother cow and her calf who had decided that the tracks were a fine place to spend the night.

Hidden in the shadows, I noticed that one of the train's car doors was ajar. *Hmm,* I thought to myself.

15

This train is headed North—the same direction I'm headed. Why don't I just hitch myself a ride?

Making a dash for it (I'm rather speedy), I hoisted myself up and into the train, gently sliding the heavy door closed. Absolute blackness. The car smelled of wood and leather and was so cozy that almost as soon as the train began to move, I was asleep.

Three

"Now what do we have here?" asked a man with a chubby black face. "A stowaway?"

I was up on my feet in a flash. "I'm sorry, Mister!" I pleaded in my best little-boy-lost voice. "I didn't hurt anything. I just needed a place to sleep. Please don't throw me off the train!" I added this last bit because I could feel that the train was now zipping along quite quickly.

"First off," said the chubby face, "no one's going to throw you off anywhere. And secondly, cut the *mister* jazz and called me by my name: Rex. What's your name, son?"

"Danny."

"Well, Daniel, I'm not going to hurt you, but Rabbit will whup your behind if he catches you near his saxophone."

And that's how I met my pal, Rex.

Since I hadn't eaten in a while, I guess I wobbled a bit.

"Are you alright?" asked Rex.

"Just a little hungry."

"Well, come on then! Let's go meet the Duke. He's eating breakfast right now and if we don't hightail it, there won't be any food left for us!"

Figuring that Rex must be the man-servant to some English toff, I said, "Can you understand him with the accent and all?"

Rex chuckled in that deep-chested way of his. "Sure, I can. Being a Washingtonian myself, I can understand the local *patois*." Seeing my confused face, he said, "Daniel, my friend, you are traveling in style with Duke Ellington and His Famous Orchestra. Step into the dining car, Sir!"

Now I knew who Duke Ellington was. Granny had owned a Victrola and four 78s: Bessie Smith's "Mean Old Bedbug Blues"; Louis Armstrong's "West End Blues"; and two by Duke: "Solitude" and "East St. Louis Toodle-Oo." I loved them all.

Finding myself stepping into a sunlit car, full of the smells of bacon and coffee, I wondered if I were perhaps dreaming. Many men, all black like me, along with one lovely coffee-colored lady, sat at tables, eating and talking and laughing. The countryside rolling past the windows was green and thick with trees.

"Duke, look what I found," said Rex. "A little stow-away hiding in the baggage car! His name's Dan and he's so hungry he almost began gnawing on Rabbit's saxophone."

A little man seated nearby lifted his hat, eyeballing me suspiciously.

"Greetings, fine lad," said one of the smoothest voices I'd ever heard. Granny would've said it was *as smooth as buttered caramel.* "Sit down, please. Would you like some breakfast?"

"Yes, Sir," I said.

Wrapped in a royal-blue bathrobe, Duke was a husky man with kind, almond-shaped eyes—eyes that seemed to dig deep into you, sizing you up with remarkable accuracy. In all the years I knew him, I never knew Duke's mind to take a break—not even for a second. (Even when he slept, Duke's fine mind was conjuring up blues, blues, and more blues). His mustache was so slight that I wondered why he'd bothered to grow it.

"Then sit down, sit down. Jonesy!" Duke called to a tiny man who came running. "Fix the lad here a plate of—how does eggs and bacon sound, with steak on the side?"

"Sounds fine to me," I said.

Duke's almond eyes were now grazing over me with amusement, it seemed. Actually, Duke gazed at the world with amusement. The only time this amusement took a vacation was when he dove into composing music—and then the world was tuned out and nothing mattered but the notes he'd be scribbling onto envelopes, gum wrappers, menus—anything that he could get his hands on.

While I stuffed myself, Duke and the lovely coffee-colored lady—her name was Ivie—asked me the questions you'd expect: *How old are you? Where are you from? Do you have any family? Where are you headed?* (My answers, by the way, were *Nine; Helen, Georgia; Not anymore; Don't have a clue*).

"Jonesy," said Duke with a chuckle. "This lad's appetite rivals my own; fill up his plate." As I dove in for seconds, he continued: "We're playing a concert in Washington tonight and then we're heading home to Harlem for a few weeks before heading out to California, playing one-nighters the entire way. You don't play any instrument, do you?"

"No, Sir."

"That's no matter. I travel with enough temperamental *artistes*. Now I don't know how this grabs you, Daniel, but you're welcome to travel with us up to New York City. There's an extra bedroom in my apartment in Harlem, plenty of room on this train, and you can earn your keep by . . . I don't know . . . carrying a few suitcases here and there. Sound good?"

Needless to say, it did.

And that's how I joined Duke's band of merry men—and, of course, Ivie.

Four

Now's a good time to fill you in on the musicians in Duke's band. Some I grew to know well, while others stuck to themselves. These ones were never mean to me—who'd be mean to a kid?—but apart from the odd grunted request (*Hey, kid, could you find me a match?)* they didn't have much to do with me.

Rex: My pal and teacher, Duke's cornet player. When Rex threw books my way, like *David Copperfield,* you better be sure that I read them. I wouldn't be writing this story if it weren't for Rex's encouragement.

Rabbit: Short, suspicious of strangers, and very quiet, Rab was Duke's alto sax man. (His real name was Johnny Hodges). Looking almost bored on stage, when he played a solo you could hear those ladies sighing from clear across town. And when Rabbit blew the blues . . . man, you could feel *those* notes in the deepest part of your soul.

Sonny: Duke's tall, pop-eyed, crazy drummer man. Sonny's mouth, since he talked in his sleep, ran twenty-four hours a day. When we were in England, Sonny wore a bowler hat everywhere and called everyone, male or female, *chap*.

Harry: Almost as big as his sound on the baritone sax, Harry was my pal. Just a wink from him would tell me not to worry, that everything would be alright. Harry was a kind, dignified, *together* man.

Barney: Duke's bald-headed clarinet man from New Orleans, Barney was a thoughtful dude who lived for his music and his red beans and rice.

Jimmy: A tall, quiet boy who looked like an Indian, Jimmy lived for his bass. His never-ending coughing, though, could climb on one's nerves.

Tricky Sam: A sleepy-lidded card shark, Tricky could make his trombone speak, *yah, yah, yah, yah.* . . . Placing a small cylinder of metal in his horn's bell, he'd then wave a (clean) rubber toilet plunger over the bell to make voice-like *wah-wah/yah-yah* sounds. Sam's musical voices could sound sly and tricky, or low-down-somebody-just-died mournful. Like Rex, Tricky Sam loved books—especially those about his main man Marcus Garvey or his beloved West Indies heritage.

Juan and Lawrence: Duke's other trombone men. Since Juan always carried a knife, I kept my distance.

Juan was born in Puerto Rico, so his complexion was lighter than the rest of ours. One night in Texas a sheriff "urged" him to darken his face with make-up "so it won't look like ya'll has a white boy in with you coloreds." Lawrence, as tall and almost as good-looking as Duke, was nicknamed "the Deacon" because he carried himself like a man of the cloth. For some reason, we were shy in each other's company and so avoided each other. A shame.

Otto: Bald as an egg and almost as crazy as Sonny, Otto played several instruments with plenty of vigor, and had been friends with Duke for years.

Cootie: A proud, dignified artist from Mobile, Alabama, Cootie played a blazing trumpet—which with the help of a mute became a growling jungle cat.

Jonesy: Duke's diminutive right-hand man, always ready with a light or a lift. He was responsible for setting up (and polishing) Sonny's massive drum kit—at least until I took over.

Ivie: a beautiful, kindhearted lady who always made sure that I was comfortable, well-fed or both. I always tried to be around when Ivie sang "Stormy Weather" with so much feeling that it made me ache. Yup, I was in love with her, but I knew that to her I'd always be a kid brother. She was one of the most beautiful women I've ever known.

Duke: Hmm, now there's a tough one. Sorry, but I

can't sum up the Duke. As friendly as could be, generous too, but always keeping people at a distance, always living inside his head. Maybe that's what geniuses do—live inside their own minds, creating their art.

•   •   •   •

Later that same day, around four in the afternoon, Duke's train pulled into Union Station in Washington, D.C. For me, who had never ventured out of Georgia since Granny found me, it was all like a dream. The station's ceiling rose higher than the tallest trees back home. Hundreds of folks—men in baggy suits, women in snazzy dresses—rushed hither and thither.

"You can earn your keep, Daniel," said Duke, "by loading some of our instruments into that truck you see out through those doors. Just be gentle with those horns. Rabbit will skin you alive if you harm his axe."

Back in the baggage car, Jonesy and several porters were already lugging the various saxophones and trumpets and trombones through the crowd to the waiting truck. I was just about to (cleverly) pick up a sax smaller than the others when a hand darted past and nabbed it first.

"Nothing personal," said Rabbit with a thin grin, "but I'm the only man who carries my horn. Here, take this snare drum instead. Sonny's not so particular."

Hearing coughing, I turned to see Jimmy—a slender boy with a boy's mustache—amble into the car.

25

Nodding politely, he headed toward an instrument, nestled inside a black bag, that was taller than I was. "And I'm the only one who carries my bass," he said. "The name's Jimmy. Nice to meet you, kid." Another cough seized him.

"Are you alright?" I asked.

"Yeah, fine." His eyes were moist from the coughing fit.

"Have you been with Duke long?" I asked.

Jimmy grinned. "About ten months. Crazy story. One night I was jamming in a club in St. Louis. It was late—about two in the morning. I look out and there's the famous Rex Stewart, Duke Ellington's cornettist. I can't believe my eyes! But then he's gone. I figured he wasn't too impressed. But about ten minutes later he returns—with Duke Ellington in tow! And get this: Duke's wearing his blue bathrobe and slippers! 'You gotta hear this kid,' I hear Rex say. About fifteen minutes later Duke asked me if I wanted to join. It was like a dream. Still is. See you at the theater, kid." Jimmy carefully stepped out the train's door, through the crowd, hailed a cab, and he and his bass were gone.

"Oh, Daniel." It was Duke, carrying three suitcases. "Would you mind grabbing one of these? Many thanks." Juggling a snare drum and a suitcase, I headed toward the station door with Duke Ellington. A red-faced policeman, leaning against a pole, toothpick in the corner of his mouth, said, "Duke, if you'd been born a white man, you'd've been one great musician."

His face tightening, Duke smiled that mysterious smile of his, glanced at the cop, and said, "No doubt my life *would* have been different had I been born a white man." The cop looked perplexed.

A few minutes later, in the back seat of a taxi, Jonesey said: "Man, I wanted to smack that cop right in the puss."

Looking out the window, that dreamy look in his eye, Duke said: "And what's the point of that, J? You'll be tossed in a jail cell and forgotten. Nah, I'll simply take my righteous anger and write a few blues with it. Look up ahead, Daniel. That's the White House. My father worked there when I was a boy."

I was speechless. To think that only last evening I'd been tramping the red-dirt paths of Georgia . . . and here . . . half a day later . . . I was gazing at the home of President Roosevelt, its many flags flapping in the warm May sunshine! Duke dutifully pointed out the Capital and the various monuments to me. And the cars! I think I saw more of them, all black, in ten minutes than I had in my entire life.

"With whom should the young sprite room?" asked Duke.

"How about Rabbit?" chuckled Jonesy.

"No, I was thinking about Jimmy."

"Think about the cough, though."

"That's true. I got it! Rex! He still owes me for saving his life in the municipal pool." Duke winked at me. "I tell him that I don't remember that day—but of course I do. It's not every day that one saves another's life. Fat Stuff was sinking like a safe."

"Do you like to read?" asked Jonesy.

"Sure. Granny was always taking out books from our church library for me to read."

Duke slapped his hands together. "So that settles it. You're rooming with Fat Stuff."

• • • •

The hotel was in the black quarter of Washington, far indeed from the White House, but the sheets were clean and fresh air blew in through its open windows. Rex was asleep, snoring up a storm on his side of the room. I'd just finished washing my face in the sink in the corner when someone tapped lightly on the door. It was Ivie.

"Do you have any change of clothes in that smelly gunny sack of yours?" she whispered.

"Just a few, Ma'am."

"Don't *ma'am* me, boy. I'm only old enough to be your slightly older sister. Well, what're you waiting for? Come on, then!"

For the next few hours Ivie led me from store to store, buying me shirts, pants, pajamas, shoes, and underclothes. In a musty, dusty second hand shop she bought me a fine leather satchel, big enough to hold my new gear. Afterwards we stopped at a café for some coffee.

"You really have no one to call your own?" she asked, her big beautiful eyes filling with tears for me.

"No, Ma'am—" (just as quickly those eyes flashed anger in my direction)—"I mean *Ivie*. It was just me and Granny, and I knew that one day she'd be hitting the sky."

"And how old are you?"

"I was born on November 30, 1927, Granny always told me. So I'm still nine, but I'll be ten before Christmas."

Ivie smiled and her smile was as beautiful as her eyes. "Well, you've landed with a good crew. Duke has a heart of gold and so do his men. Just don't go messin' with Rabbit's saxophone and you'll be alright." She laughed. "Oh, yes, and don't fall into a poker game with either Tricky Sam or myself or we'll skin you alive." Again, that glorious laugh. "Other than that, you're in safe territory. I expect that Rex will have you reading all sorts of books on all sorts of subjects, but there's certainly no harm in that."

"Thanks for the clothes, Ivie," I said. "I'll pay you back as soon as I can."

She laid her soft hand on top of mine. "Hey, I won

the money fair and square last night playing poker—and I'll win just as much tonight on the train, so there's no worries, Dannyboy, no worries."

• • • •

The theater was dark and echoey. I stood on its stage, gazing out at the endless rows of plush red seats.

"Yep, this theater's a beauty, ain't she?" said a big-eyed, smiling man. "I always love playing the Howard." He stuck out a bony hand. "I'm Sonny. I can't find Jonesy anywhere. Care to help me set up my drums?"

It took a while, but his immense kit was finally assembled. By this time the stage had filled up with the instruments and musicians of Duke's band. Several, including Rex and Rabbit, were enjoying a little jam session in a darkened corner of the stage. Sorry to be corny, but this music made me glad to be sharing the earth with the people who created it.

The slender boy, Jimmy, was quietly tuning up his bass.

"Hey," I said.

"Hey yourself, kid. Man, I got *big* eyes for those clothes! You're looking *slick*."

"Thanks. Ivie bought them for me."

"Man, how do you rate?" he asked with a laugh. "She's never even bought me a piece of *thread*, let alone clothes that tasty!"

Around six o'clock a scrumptious meal of hot chicken gumbo, Maryland crab cakes, and corn-on-the-cob was delivered backstage. As I ate and laughed and talked with the musicians, they made me feel like I truly belonged.

"Dannyboy," said a large man with a calm, kind face. "Once you're finished scarfing down all that food, come see me."

Dinner finished, I stood alone on the stage. All of the musicians' instruments were waiting in their stands, gleaming and silent. A few early customers were finding their seats.

"Hey, I'm coming to you instead," called the large man, walking slowly across the polished wooden floor, extending a bear paw. "My name's Harry. My instrument is the baritone sax. Have you ever played an instrument before?"

"No, Sir," I said.

"Well, try this baby out," said Harry, handing me a silver trumpet. "It's one of Cootie's old ones."

I was surprised: the trumpet was lighter than it looked. Raising it to my lips, I fully expected to hear sweet, mellow music. Instead, I heard a dozen geese being savagely strangled. My cheeks collapsed, the spittle flew, and I gave up.

Harry chuckled. "Now that wasn't too bad—it was *worse* than too bad! Cootie or Rex will have to give you some lessons. But the trumpet's yours if you want it."

I couldn't believe my ears. Like all of the boys back home, I wanted to learn how to play trumpet like our idol, Louis Armstrong.

"Sure," said Harry. "But don't thank me—it was Cootie's idea."

"Which one's Cootie?" I asked. "I haven't met him yet."

"Don't you worry," said Harry. "You will."

•   •   •   •

The stage curtains were now closed. The murmurings of the audience grew louder by the moment. One by one the musicians, now decked out in fancy red jackets and black slacks, strolled onto the stage, some laughing, some talking quietly. I stood out of the way, watching. Each musician seemed to have his own ritual to prepare himself for the performance. Some fingered their horns and silently blew. Others cleaned and polished. Jimmy gave his bass a thorough going over with a red cloth. Ivie, looking more than lovely in a white gown, seemed to me to be praying. Duke was nowhere in sight.

Suddenly—darkness!—the lights zapped off and a voice from somewhere said, "Ladies and gentlemen, please give a warm Washington welcome to our hometown hero, Mr. Duke Ellington, and his Famous Orchestra!" The applause exploded, the curtain opened, the stage was bathed in blue light, and I felt Duke breeze by.

A swirl of piano notes floated past, the band kicked in, and I spent the next two hours with my mouth wide open. (I could almost hear Granny's voice: *"You, boy, shut your mouth before it becomes a flea hive!"*). Suddenly Ivie was standing next to me. "This song is called *Rockin' in Rhythm*," she explained.

"It sure does," I said, before asking, "When do you sing?"

"In a little while," she replied, a dreamy look on her face. Even after years with Duke, she obviously enjoyed hearing this music as much as I did.

Song after song passed by like music from an unforgettable dream. The upbeat numbers roared. I could feel Sonny's drums and Jimmy's bass in my throat and chest. In one song Rabbit, his face impassive, stood up to solo, and the sound from his saxophone was as slow and sweet as poured honey. Some ladies were shouting out loud, like in church back home. "That was Johnny Hodges, folks," said Duke as the applause finally died down, "smelting the melody to smoldering."

"Sometimes I don't know *what* that man is on about," said Ivie, "but I still love to hear him talk!"

"And now, ladies and gentlemen," said Duke from the stage, "please give a warm Howard Theater welcome to our singer, the lovely and vivacious . . . *Ivie Anderson!*"

Punching me on the shoulder, Ivie said, "Here I go!" and then seemingly floated to the microphone. Her first song was an upbeat one, "Rose of the Rio Grande," followed by a song Granny used to hum while sweeping up, "Stormy Weather." Looking over, Ivie shot me a wink and a smile.

"For *years* I've been trying to get that woman to notice me," said a voice behind me. It was Jonesy. "Now *you* just waltz in and *boom!* you've got her winking at you left, right, and center. What's your secret, kid?"

"Just a lucky so-and-so, I guess."

All too soon the curtain was closed and the show was over. The applause roared on and on, but the men had already begun packing up their instruments.

"Let's try to be on the train by midnight, everyone," said Duke.

"But what about our hotel room?" I asked Rex, who was emptying his cornet of spit.

"Oh, that was just for our afternoon nap. Don't worry, though, your fine new satchel and fancy threads were all packed up by yours truly and will be safely ensconced on the train."

I almost asked Rex what *ensconced* meant, but then figured it must mean *tucked in*, so I kept my mouth shut.

Earning my keep, I helped by carrying Sonny's cymbals and later Harry's saxophone to a waiting truck. I thought of asking Rabbit if I could carry *his* sax, but then thought better of it. (*How can a man play such beautiful music on his horn*, I wondered, *while looking like he's thinking of last month's rainfall?*)

An hour later, as Duke's silver train pulled out of Union Station, a huge meal of roast beef, mashed potatoes, and collard greens was served in the dining car.

"Hey, Dan," said Rabbit, "I've got an old pair of pajamas that I'll cut down. They should fit you."

He can be friendly, I thought.

"Don't worry yourself, Rab," said Tricky Sam. "Ivie's done gone and bought the boy a spanking new pair. He doesn't need *your* hand-me-downs."

A chorus of laughs and catcalls and whistles accompanied this bit of news. Ivie, eating with one hand and holding her poker cards with the other, simply smiled slow and lazy.

Soon I was washed up and in my new blue-striped pajamas.

"Where am I sleeping?" I asked Rex.

"Just so happens that there are two extra berths. Would you prefer the top or the bottom?"

I had always dreamed of sleeping on a train. "I'll take the top."

Climbing up, I snuggled under the covers. The

sheets felt crisp and clean, like the way Granny kept ours at home.

"Here, let me tuck you in," said Ivie, kissing me on the forehead. "Sleep tight, little man."

From down the hallway I could hear Jonesy's voice: "Aw, *maaaan*! What's the kid's *secret*?"

"He's cute—*and* a gentleman," replied Ivie. "You grunts should be taking notes."

One by one the musicians climbed into their berths; the hall lights were switched off. Someone somewhere was softly playing a piano. I tried to think back over the day—of meeting Rex in the baggage car, of shopping with Ivie, of Duke's glorious music—but with the *click-click-clicking* of the rails and the occasional wail of the train's whistle, I was soon lost in sleep.

Five

"Hey, Dannyboy, wake up! We're in Grand Central Station!"

I opened my eyes to Harry's beaming, boyish face. Our sleeping car was sleeping no longer.

"Come on, Daniel!" said Rex. "Harry and I are going to give you our Grade A tour of New York City and believe me, Georgia boy, your eyes are going to see such sights!"

In a few moments I found myself in the largest room I'd ever seen, staring at a blue ceiling high, high above. People of all shapes and sizes were rushing to and fro. You'd think that such a busy place would be noisy beyond belief, but this place wasn't—just a whispery, cavernous *whoosh*.

"Look, Rex," I said, "there's stars up in the ceiling!"

"Yup, this is Grand Central, the finest station in all the world," said Rex. "You are in the Big Apple now, Daniel!"

Duke, dressed in a natty blue suit, strolled up. "You're coming with me now, Dan. You can wash up and meet my sister, Ruth, and later on these ruffians can swing by to show you the town. Unfortunately, they know where I live."

Within five minutes, Duke and I were in the back-seat of a taxicab. Another cab, filled with Duke's luggage (and my one bag), followed behind.

"Turn around, son," said Duke. "We're on Fifth Avenue and if you look back you'll see the Empire State Building. Look real close and you'll see King Kong's footprints."

"Couldn't they wash 'em off?" I asked, suddenly realizing the true meaning of the word *skyscraper*. Duke only chuckled.

As the cab rolled up the avenue, I swung my head left, right, backwards, forwards, trying to take it all in. *I'm in New York City!* I told myself, only halfway believing it. *There are more people here in a single block than in the entire town of Helen!*

It was a warm May morning and the open cab windows brought in the smells of diesel and burning pretzels. Hundreds of people were out and about, waiting for the traffic lights to change over here, hustling across the street over there. Almost all of the men wore loosely cut suits and hats. The women wore brightly colored dresses that swung in the morning breeze. A beautiful green park was on our left, with stone buildings fit for royalty on our right. In the park, women pushed strollers, children yelled and played, and old men sat on benches. The sun made deep cool shadows on the pavement. I saw black folks and white folks, mingling together, although further up the avenue there were more and more black folks.

"That's Central Park," explained Duke, "and we're now in Harlem. I live in a section of Harlem called Sugar Hill. If you ever get lost, simply ask for Duke's place on Edgecombe Avenue. I live with my sister Ruth and my son, Mercer. How old are you again?"

"Nine."

"Mercer's eighteen. He's a fine trumpeter and he's becoming quite the arranger, too, I'm proud to say. He'll be traveling with the band across the country this summer. We'll be in California for a month, then we'll do another Southern swing."

"Don't you ever just sit still, Duke?" I asked.

Again that chuckle. "Not if I can help it."

Soon the taxi turned off Fifth Avenue onto a quiet, tree-lined street of brick apartment buildings. Here, up in Harlem, nearly all the folks going about their business were as black as me.

"Right here, driver," said Duke.

Duke's building, a seven-story beauty, was at 381

39

Edgecombe Avenue. In the lobby a uniformed man actually saluted him. "How was the trip, Duke? Did you knock 'em dead down South?"

"Some of them, Eddie, some of them. Meet our new friend, Danny."

I shook old Eddie's gnarled hand. "Nice to meet you, Sir."

"You, too, son. Are you a musician?"

"Not yet, Eddie," said Duke, "but one never knows. Right now he'll be carrying bags and lifting saxes and polishing Sonny's drums."

We took the elevator to the third floor, where Duke's apartment was filled with sunshine and smelled like flowers. A beautiful young woman, Duke's sister Ruth, greeted her brother with a hug and me with a smile.

"Welcome home, Edward! And is this the hitch-hiker you mentioned in your telegram?"

"The very same. He stowed away on our train somewhere in Georgia and we all like him, so it looks like we're stuck with him. Daniel, I'm proud to say that this lovely young woman is my sister, Ruth."

I reached out my hand, but Ruth swooped me up in a bear hug. "Let me show you to your room, Danny. We always keep it ready for any guests who might pop by."

I had to keep my mouth from popping open too

wide. My new bedroom was almost as big as Granny's cottage. Outside its four windows stood leafy green trees filled with springtime birds. In the distance shimmered the skyscrapers of New York. Like the rest of the apartment, the room was filled with sunshine. Laying my new satchel on a large oak desk, I could only stare and whistle.

Duke strolled in. "Not bad, eh? You have your own bathroom beyond that door, so feel free to take a shower. Ruth, do we have an extra toothbrush lying around?"

"I think I can dig one up. Are you two hungry? I'll make some lunch."

Back home we had a rusty washtub and once a week, usually on Saturday nights, Granny would heat up some water and scrub my back with her harsh, pig-bristled brush. Here I stepped into a shower stall and hot water flowed out of the spigot—all I could ever want or need! And I'm not even mentioning the sweet smelling soaps and shampoos and the thick, soft towels! Needless to say, after drying off, brushing my teeth, and stepping into some of the sharp new duds that Ivie had bought for me, I felt like Prince Danny of Harlem himself!

For a spell, I leaned on the window sill in my new bedroom—a big butternut tree right outside, tossing its shade around left, right, and center. Watching the citizens of Harlem parading past—well-dressed women holding their children's hands; office girls on their lunch break; workmen in overalls; men in crisp suits; a policeman on horseback; young girls strolling and laughing—I thought to myself: *Remember this moment. It's May, 1937, and you're in Sugar Hill in Harlem. Remember this moment!*

And I always have.

Ruth had whipped up tuna fish sandwiches for lunch and I munched while she and Duke gossiped. I'd just taken a last bite when a car horn honked from below. "Hey, Dannyboy!" called Harry. "Let's go! New York City is waiting for you!"

"You're in for a treat," said Ruth, returning from the window. "A tour of the city with Harry and Rex. Just don't lead those two altar boys astray, you hear?"

"And tell them to be at the Apollo by six o'clock," said Duke, his mouth full of sandwich. "I want to rehearse a few new numbers before our show."

"Okay, bye! Thanks for lunch, Ruth!" Eddie was waiting by the elevator doors and in a few moments I was in the backseat of Harry's shiny black convertible, a springtime breeze blowing by.

"Duke said to be at the Apollo by six. What's the Apollo?" I asked.

Rex turned around. "You've never heard of it? Man, it's the biggest theater in Harlem and we practically own the joint. You should hear the ladies moan when I play my horn!"

"Yeah," said Harry, "moaning with pain."

Harry drove down Fifth Avenue, with Central Park now on our right. Sitting back, I breathed in deeply and enjoyed the ride. Soon the park was past and both sides of the avenue were lined with buildings. "Look on your left, Dan," said Harry. "That's St. Patrick's Cathedral—man, it's beautiful inside. We should stop in sometime. You religious?"

"No, Baptist," I said.

"Me, too," said Harry, "but it doesn't make much difference, does it? God's everywhere. Like Duke says: 'Each person prays in his or her own language and there isn't a language that God doesn't understand.'"

"Thanks for the sermon, Reverend," said Rex. "Look on your right, Daniel. That's Rockefeller Center. Seems like just yesterday that it was a hole in the ground."

At a red light three beautiful girls, their spring skirts swirling, crossed in front of the car. "It's Harry and Rex from Duke's band!" squealed one, and they all waved. "Where are you fellas playing these days?"

"You lovely ladies hop on up to the Apollo tonight and we'll play just for you," said Rex with a wink. Reaching into his shirt pocket, he pulled out three tickets and handed them over. "See you there!" The light changed and Harry drove on. "Hey!" he said. "Let's take the lad to the top of the Empire State Building!"

The elevator in the world's tallest building made my stomach dip and my ears pop. In a few minutes I was standing at the railing, staring out at this unbelievable city.

"What a day!" said Harry, his broad face beaming. "Now look over to your right—that's the East River. See that stone bridge way down there? That's the Brooklyn Bridge. Ivie loves to take walks over it—maybe she'll bring you one day. Now see up there? That's Central Park and way up there is Harlem and Duke's apartment."

Like excited little boys, Harry and Rex led me to the other side of the observatory.

"Now *that's* the Hudson River," said Rex. "Can you see that ocean liner down there in dock? We took one like that to England with Duke a few years back. Now on the other side of the Hudson is New Jersey. Just step over here . . . that's right. Way down there is Greenwich Village. Jimmy and Rabbit and Harry and I go down there and jam some nights. A lot of painters and poets live there, and skin color don't seem to matter. Now look way, way out. See out there in the harbor?"

I was excited, too. "Is that the Statue of Liberty?" I asked.

"You bet," said Rex, "and that's where we're headed!"

I couldn't believe how my life had changed since I'd jumped that train. Here I was, gazing out on Manhattan on this May morning. The cars below—except for the yellow taxis, all black—seemed smaller than toys . . . smoke billowed out of dozens of chimneys and from a tugboat chugging slowly up the East River . . . wooden water towers stood on many of the roofs . . . I could see a woman staring out of a window far below . . . the sky was an ocean blue, with a few wispy clouds sailing along . . . an airplane floated lazily above the city, droning like an insect. . . .

This is perfect, I thought.

• • • •

Later, in a shady park surrounded by water, Harry treated us to hotdogs and root beer. "This is Battery Park," he explained. "It's the very tip of Manhattan island. Look out there, Dan: There's Lady Liberty herself. If we're hungry later, old Rex can treat us to more hotdogs out on her island."

"Be glad to," said Rex.

Seagulls dipped and glided overhead. I was jealous of the ones who were riding pockets of smooth air over the choppy waters.

"What do you call that big horn you play, Harry?" I asked.

"That's a baritone sax. Duke says I'm the band's solid foundation, keeping everything grounded."

Rex's mouth was filled with hotdog. "I heartily concur, Sir," he said.

"Have you been with Duke long?"

Harry smiled his wide, peaceful smile. "Eleven years," he said proudly. "I was so young when I left Boston to go with Duke that my mama had to write a letter giving him permission to take me on the road! Going to Harlem back then was like traveling to the ends of the earth. Little did I know that I'd go all over the country and even to Europe with Duke. Breathe in deeply, Danny. You can smell the Atlantic."

On the ferry ride out to Liberty Island, I found that Rex had joined Duke's orchestra in 1934. "Get this: I was the man who replaced Louis Armstrong in the Fletcher Henderson Orchestra! Talk about pressure! But playing with Duke has been nothing but pleasure. Sadly, I joined too late for the '33 trip to Europe, but I keep bugging Duke to go back over."

Harry, shielding his eyes with one hand, was staring out over the sun-drenched waves. "World's getting too dangerous, Rex. I just want to stay here in the good old U.S. of A."

Soon we were stepping off the ferry. "You know, I never pictured the statue green," I said.

"She can't hold her liquor," said Harry.

"Not bad," chuckled Rex.

Suddenly, with the sunshine, and huge Lady Liberty in front of me, and the stony buildings of Manhattan behind me, I felt this crazy burst of energy. It felt incredible to be running with the salty wind in my face.

"Come on!" I yelled back to Rex and Harry.

"We've got a lot of blowing to do tonight," grumbled Rex. "We can't be running all over creation, boy."

Up and up the staircase we climbed (me up ahead naturally), higher and higher into the statue. Harry was mopping his face with a polka-dotted handkerchief. "This is hotter than Mobile in July," he muttered. "Cootie would feel right at home here."

Finally we stood by a row of dusty little windows—the jewels in the statue's crown. "Will you look at that!" I said.

Sunlight blazed off the waters of New York Harbor. A deep rumble seemed to echo in my chest: It was the ocean liner we had seen from the Empire State Building, now heading for open sea. Gulls whirled above the statue's head and perched on her torch.

"Lord, will you look at that!" whispered Rex.

"Haven't you been up here before?"

"No—we're usually sleeping during the day," said Rex, "and playing all night long."

We enjoyed another hot dog or three stretched out

on the lawn by the water. It was chilly on the ferry ride back to Manhattan and I must have fallen asleep in the back seat of Harry's car.

"Hey, wake up, Dannyboy," called Harry from a long way away. "You're back in Sugar Hill."

Yawning, I stretched. "Thanks for the tour, guys."

"Our pleasure, Daniel," said Rex.

"See you at the Apollo tonight!" said Harry before speeding off.

Ruth opened the apartment door. "Enjoy the ride?" she asked.

"I loved it, but this city can tire a body out. Do you mind if I take a nap, Ruth?"

"This is your new home, Dan, so make yourself comfortable. My brother certainly does—he's been sleeping all day!"

Late afternoon shadows were spilling across my bedroom floor. The occasional automobile horn below sounded muffled and distant. Birds were twittering in the branches outside the window. In no time I was asleep.

Six

"Hello," said a voice.

Opening my eyes, I wasn't quite sure where I was.

"I'm Mercer," said a young man with an open, friendly face. "I'm Ellington's son." He stuck out his hand. "Nice to meet you. Ruth says it's time to eat."

Across the street, the red bricks of an apartment building were orangey with late afternoon sun. I could see a man sitting by a window in his shirt sleeves, reading a newspaper.

Mercer smiled. "Ellington told me how you all met. Very resourceful on your part."

After washing up, I followed the delicious smells to the dining room. Duke was up, dressed only in a blue bathrobe, already digging into the grub.

"Daniel, Daniel, Daniel," he said, his mouth full. "Sit down and pitch in before I eat it all!"

Ruth had cooked up quite a meal: roast beef,

mashed potatoes, green beans, hot dinner rolls, and honey-glazed carrots. You can be sure that I dug in with all of my might, but I was like a gnat compared with Duke—helping after helping of the beef and fixings, all washed down with hot black coffee. You probably won't believe me, but his dessert was three bowls of coffee ice cream and four slices of apple pie! Afterwards, he sat back, sipped his coffee, and smiled.

"I have to say, Daniel, that eating is one of my vocations—along with tinkling on the piano and traveling the world with my band of expensive gentlemen. Mercer here can't decide if he'll be joining us on our trek to California."

Mercer shrugged. "I'm in two city baseball leagues and I want to finish my seasons. Nothing personal."

I noticed that Mercer called his father *Ellington* behind his back but *Pop* to his face. I almost asked where Mercer's mother was at, but I decided to keep my mouth shut. Besides, the long slashing scar on Duke's right cheek was probably announcing a thing or two about his married state.

Fixing me with those almond eyes (which usually seemed to be mocking the world), Duke said: "When my mother passed away two years ago, I was bereft. Ruth and Mercer will both tell you that I was as useless as a screen door on a submarine."

"He's not lying," said Ruth.

"So it's been only days since *your* grandmother died, Daniel. Why are you so chipper?"

I had been wondering the same thing, to tell you the truth. "Well. . . ," I said, simply to buy time, ". . . I think Granny was always talking so much about the next world—*I'll be there soon, Danny, and I'll try to look out for you*, she'd say—that I'd gotten used to the idea. Sometimes when she'd be cooking she'd suddenly grab her chest and say, 'Someone just walked over my grave.' So when she finally did take off into the wild blue yonder, I wasn't so shocked. Then, of course, I've met all of *you* fine folk and seen Washington and now New York, so I really haven't had much time to grieve. But don't get me wrong—I loved Granny. She was the only family I've ever known."

Reaching over, Duke patted the top of my hand. "I asked a sensitive question and I received a sensitive reply. Anything you wish to ask me?"

There was. "How do they put that music of yours on those 78 discs? Back home Granny and I almost wore out your tune 'Solitude'—and I always wondered how the music is trapped on that shellac."

"Ah, *Solitude*," mused Duke. "I wrote that in ten minutes in a recording studio, waiting for the engineers to mike up Sonny's drums. Someday you'll have to accompany the band into the recording studio and we'll show you how the trick is done." He looked at his watch. "And our trick now is to be at the Apollo in fifteen minutes. I'm going to brush my teeth. Mercer, could you please call a cab?"

"Sure, Pop."

It was a cool night and the street lamps cast long leafy shadows across the sidewalks. Duke chatted up front with the driver, while Mercer and I sat in the back. "When we turn the corner," said Mercer, "we'll be on 125th Street, the main drag of Harlem."

I'd never seen so bright a sight since the carnival had come to town when I was six. The citizens of Harlem—freshly bathed and dressed to perfection, laughing, smiling—strolled past, mingled in small groups, or sat on the evening stoops. The taxi windows were open wide and somewhere good food was cooking. And the music!—pouring from every bar and dance hall. It was Friday night and a distinct feeling of celebration was in the air.

From several blocks away I could read the Apollo's blazing neon marquee: *Tonight and Saturday! They're home! Duke Ellington and His Famous Orchestra!* An immense crowd, snaking up 125th Street, was already waiting.

"Let's head in the back," said Duke, instructing the driver to head over to 126th Street.

After Duke paid the one dollar fare with a ten dollar bill, the three of us headed down a dark alley. Up ahead someone was playing a blazing trumpet. With a nod, Duke disappeared through a door.

"Hey, Cootie!" said Mercer. "How was the trip?"

"Ah, you know the South, Mercer," said Cootie, wiping his mouth with his sleeve. "Nothing's changed. Hey, Dannyboy, I don't see the horn I gave you."

I felt terrible. "I'm sorry. I forgot it back at Duke's place. I can go back and—"

"It's no trouble, son," said Cootie, who had a sweet Southern twang to his voice, just like me. "I'm a bit busy anyway. Duke wants me to play a new number he's calling *Concerto for Cootie* and I've got to practice, so there's no time for a lesson now anyway. But me and Rex want to start right in on you, boy, so bring your horn tomorrow and we'll begin. How has the arranging been coming along, Mercer?"

"Beautiful, Coots. I have a new arrangement of *Echoes of Harlem* that you've *got* to hear."

"Bring it to tomorrow's rehearsal—looking forward to hearing it. And now, if you two ruffians will excuse me." Raising his trumpet, Cootie began to blow, swinging silvery notes to the starry sky above.

Backstage was bustling.

"Hey, Dan! Mercer!" called Sonny, his eyes bulging. "Help me with these drums!"

"I'll see you a little later," whispered Mercer. "I've helped Sonny with his drums enough for two lifetimes!"

"So tell me, lad," said Sonny as I polished one of his golden cymbals. "Have you ever kissed a girl?"

"Yeah, two—Debby Clay and Anne Callahan."

"Good man! Now if you ever have any questions about the ladies, you can just ask old Sonny, because he's the main man when it comes to the female persuasion."

"Ha! *The Main Man of Misery*, you mean. If you listen to this turkey, Dan, you'll be lost!" It was Ivie, looking as beautiful as ever in an icy white gown. "When you need advice about a lady, you ask *another* lady—that's my advice. And with me, the advice is *free*—not dependent on how many cymbals you can shine. So don't go asking for hints from some snake in the grass drummer!"

"I'll come straight to you, Ivie," I said.

Sonny grumbled.

Ivie smiled at me. "How was your day, baby? Harry said that you had a fine old time." While I told her about our little journey, she listened, eyes all wide. If you ever notice, a person who can truly *listen* to you is as rare as a preacher at the horse races. "Well, this won't be so exciting," she said, "but my mother and I would love to have you to our home for Sunday dinner. I'll fill you in on the details later. Got to run! Behave yourself, Sonny!"

"You've got to love that woman," said the drummer after Ivie had vanished. "She sings like an angel—

and what a cook! You're in for a treat, Dannyboy. Just don't ever play poker against her—or if you do, wear two shirts, because she'll take at least one!"

Once Sonny's drums were all set up, glimmering and shimmering, I found an old wooden chair, placed it in the shadows on the side of the stage, and got all comfortable for the show ahead. And what a show it was! As soon as the red velvet curtains slid open, the Apollo audience was on its feet, cheering, whistling, dancing in the aisles and on the seats.

"Now here's Rabbit with his *specialite du lapin*," said Duke. "*Jeep's Blues!*"

Standing center stage, lit in red, Rabbit played a slow, lazy blues on his alto saxophone. In the audience the ladies swayed and rocked. "Yeah, baby!" cried a chubby woman in the front, her face bathed in perspiration.

The band played loud and fast; the band played low and slow. Ivie glided out to sing while couples held each other and danced. I watched and listened and loved every second of it. As Cootie stepped up to the microphone, blowing a tremendous blues that made the people go *Aaaah!*, I suddenly thought to myself, *This is what I want to do with my life. I want to be a musician. Now, I might not have a lick of talent, but I'm going to give it a bash.* Song after song rolled by and I imagined myself on stage, taking part in each one. *Rex and Cootie can teach me.*

The show rolled on well beyond the midnight hour. Everyone—Duke, his musicians, the audience, *everyone*—was sweating and beaming and *happy*. This music brought only happiness. *I'm going to at least try.*

When the red curtains were closed and the applause and whistles had finally faded, I just stood and watched. My new friends were laughing and hugging and whooping it up. Tricky Sam, the sleepy-eyed trombonist, handed me an icy bottle of root beer and I drained that baby in no time.

"That was an especially fine show, folks," said Duke, who had sweated clean through his blue suit. "Rehearsal tomorrow afternoon right here at three. I have some new pieces I want to try out."

Jimmy was rubbing down his bass with a red cloth. He looked exhausted. "Hey, Dan the man," he said.

"Great show, Jimmy," I said.

"Thanks. I thought so, too."

Rabbit rested his elbow on my head. "We're jammin' at Minton's tonight, Jim, in about an hour. I'll bring a bottle."

"What's Minton's?" I asked after Rabbit had dashed off.

A cough shook Jimmy's thin frame. "It's a club not far from here. A bunch of the guys are going to be jamming along with some of Count Basie's boys.

I'm kind of tired, but my fingers feel real strong, so I think I'll go."

"Is this as much fun as it looks?" I asked.

"You mean being a musician? Yeah, even more so probably. Hey, they don't say that we *work* music, do they? We *play* music. You don't grab a lot of shut eye, but you sure can grab some kicks. I'll catch you, kid." Hoisting his bass, he ambled off.

"What do you say, friend?" asked a yawning voice. "Want to head home?" It was Mercer.

I had to admit that I was a bit bushed myself. Even though I felt like joining the gang at Minton's, I hadn't been invited.

"Let's hoof it, though. It's a great night out there."

Outside the Apollo the streets were still jumping. Taxis zipped past and music still roared out of the bars. Somewhere nearby hamburgers were sizzling. Mercer treated me to an ice cream cone at an all-night restaurant and all too soon we had reached the apartment on Edgecombe Avenue. Sitting on the stoop, we finished our cones. A big buttery moon loomed above the apartment building across the street.

"You know, it's strange to think that that's the same moon that shines down on Georgia," I said.

"I know what you mean," said Mercer. "Sometimes I think how that same moon up there shone down on the streets of ancient Athens or Rome. Then I think how one day, when we're all gone, our great-grand-children will look up at that *same moon*. Same thing with the sun. Some Egyptian laborer had his shoulders burned four thousand years ago by the very same sun you'll look at tomorrow."

"If it's not cloudy," I had to add. "Hey, is that your dad?"

It was and Duke, after tipping the driver, joined us on the stoop. "How'd you like the show, Dan?" he asked.

I didn't quite know how to express how deeply his music had touched me. "It was fantastic, Duke," was all I said.

"How'd you like to hear a lot more of my band?"

"Sure—what do you mean?"

"We're heading cross country to California in a few weeks—we'll be gone all summer—and I don't think my expensive gentlemen (and Ivie) would ever forgive me if I didn't offer you an invitation to join us. You've made quite a few friends in a very short time."

I was glad it was dark because I could feel the tears rising to my eyes. "Thanks, Duke," was all I could say.

"That's okay, son," said Duke, wrapping an arm around my shoulders. "You're with *us* now—and we take care of our own. I'm trying to convince this son-of-a-gun here to come with us, but without success."

"Maybe next time, Pop."

"A pity," said Duke with a long yawn. "All right, gentlemen, it's late. It's time we all hit the proverbial hay."

My face washed, my teeth brushed, I knelt beside my new bed in my new bedroom and said a prayer for Granny. The sounds of the city—the occasional horn, a drunken laugh—sounded far off from high up in Sugar Hill. As I climbed beneath the crisp, clean sheets, I could hear a softly played piano from down the hall. It was Duke, composing yet another tune. Before I knew it, I was gone.

$\mathcal{S}$even

Over the next few years, although I didn't attend school, I felt like I was learning every day. Rex had me reading one book after another: modern guys like Hemingway and Fitzgerald; French dudes like Flaubert and Dumas (I forget the *pere/fil* stuff); plenty of Shakespeare, especially the tragedies; and the poetry of our own people—Langston Hughes, Countee Cullen, Zora Neale Hurston, Paul Laurence Dunbar, Claude McKay, and James Weldon Johnson. "Books are portable worlds that you can carry with you anywhere," Rex once said. "They don't need electricity and they don't need a bed for the night. And when the real world intrudes, then slap that book closed and your *other* world will wait around patiently until you're ready to dive in again. It's a perfect arrangement."

But that was only the beginning. Rex and Cootie had both taken it into their heads to make another trumpet prodigy out of me. (Rex, though, played a cornet—a smaller version of the horn). Day after day, week after week, I attacked my horn—and I enjoyed playing it, too. Now I had a decision to make: Was I going to be a blazing, brassy player like Cootie, or a mellower player like Rex (although he could make his horn wail, too, when the mood struck)? Rex's sound was as plump as his physique and as big as his heart.

"You'll find the answer," said Rex, "because a true jazz musician is playing *himself* on his instrument— and sometimes it takes a man a while to discover who he really *is*."

I found that I enjoyed the mellower, mid-range notes of the horn. I liked to play the blues and make them ache—still do. I also enjoyed finding the pretty notes on the ballads, finding new ways to *embroider* the melody. (Now *that's* a fancy word, but Granny used it all the time, and I know she'd appreciate the effort).

But, being honest, I realized that I was never going to be a supreme jazz artist. I was *good*—but no better—and the musicians in Duke's band were *all* giants.

To hear the beauty of Rex's playing, you have to check out Duke's recording of *Boy Meets Horn*, recorded on a bone-snapping-cold New York night, December 22, 1938. The snow was blowing like crazy but the studio felt cozy and warm, smelling of coffee. I was there that evening and I saw how carefully Duke monitored the placing of the microphones into which his musicians played live. Man, he had those studio cats *jumping!* (Yet he was so pleasant and unstuck up that no one seemed to mind). Behind a glass wall sat the engineer who oversaw the capturing of the music onto a master wax disc, which was the mama (or papa) of all the *other* discs that found their way across America and even overseas to many countries (much to Duke's pleasant surprise). It was fascinating to watch.

All of Rex's personality is in *Boy Meets Horn*—his sly wit; his positive view of people and the world; his good heart. Hearing it all these years later, I'm brought back to that long ago night. When the band finally emerged from the studio at around two in the morning, the snow had stopped and the stars were achingly close over the spires and peaks of Manhattan.

One night backstage I asked Rex how he achieved his unique sound on his cornet. He sounded like no one else on earth. Winking, he said, "Sometimes I only push the valves halfway down."

"But that isn't supposed to work," I said.

"I know—but I've been experimenting for months and months, and now it's working just fine."

"What did Duke say?"

Rex smiled with pride. "He was the one who encouraged me to push on with my experiment. 'It will give me yet another tonal color for my palette, Fat Stuff,' he said."

I just shook my head, having experienced enough trouble producing a non-farting sound while playing my horn the *correct* way. But that was Duke's method: He encouraged his musicians to be true individuals, even if that meant breaking a few time-honored rules along the way.

Now to hear Cootie in all *his* glory, check out *Concerto for Cootie*, recorded in Chicago on March 15, 1940. I wasn't there for that one, but I can still see Cootie on stage, hear his blazing open horn and his sly, bluesy, growling *wa-wa* when he flashed his rubber toilet plunger (I kid you not!) in front of his trumpet. Cootie hailed from Mobile, Alabama and his music was as steamy and pungent as that fine city. His sound was totally different from Rex's—but that was the point. Duke wanted each of his musicians to have his *own* sound, full of his *own* soul, and when Duke wrote his music, he wasn't writing for just saxophone or clarinet or trombone. He was writing for Rabbit's sensual, yearning cry . . . or Barney's woody, New Orleans tang . . . or Tricky Sam's humorous, winking, conversational trombone.

And every day I would practice and every now and again, when the hour was late and the dancers were tired, Duke would say from his piano, "And now, fair ladies and gallant gentlemen, here is the horn of a young man from Helen, Georgia, a young man who plays with all of the *savoir faire* and *je ne sais quoi* of his forebears. Ladies and gentlemen: *Danny Bolden.*" Thoroughly relaxed, with the golden cushion of that glorious orchestra to fall back on, I would play sad, mellow, thoughtful blues—similar to Rex's blues, but not as deep, because *I* was not yet as deep as that good man. But when the show was over, and I was helping Sonny pack up his drums, the musicians never failed to praise me and Ivie never failed to kiss me.

It was a family, all right.

It was a family that traveled mostly by train. At first I thought that Duke owned the train—but he didn't. He rented it—a dining car, where we spent most of the day; two sleeping cars; and a baggage car for the instruments, lighting and sound equipment. This was the thirties and Jim Crow—the separation of the races in everything from restaurants to schools to hospitals—was everywhere. In the South finding lodging and food was difficult, if not impossible. So Duke solved the problem with our gleaming train. "Remember, Daniel," he said to me once, "this is the way President Roosevelt travels—first class all the way."

Riding on Duke's Train

In my memories it's always night, with the dark countryside—farmland, forest, dozing little towns— hurtling past the windows. After a show we'd all be so wired that sleeping right away was out of the question. I'd grab a quick shower, change into pajamas, and try to join one of the floating poker games that were always going on. Naturally, I'd always avoid any game that included Ivie. As kind as she was, she was also a ruthless poker player who usually cleaned up, a satisfied smirk on her lovely face.

No, my poker professor was Duke's sleepy-eyed trombonist, Tricky Sam. "*Now* you've got it," he'd always say after I'd bluffed my way to a fat pile of cash. "*That's* my student." Like Rex, he was always reading, mostly books about his beloved West Indies. "I hope we get to play there one day," he'd say, a faraway look in his eyes. Like Cootie, Tricky Sam used a rubber toilet plunger as a mute to make music that sounded like conversation. "Oooooh, *yeeee-eeeees*," he'd say on his horn whenever he saw a pretty girl in the audience. Standing at the side of the stage, I'd then know to scour the crowd and, sure enough, there would be standing a "startled doe"—a true beauty.

So almost two years passed by in a blur of train travel, new cities, concerts, dances, more train travel, familiar old cities, more new cities, brief stays in Manhattan up in Sugar Hill, followed by more train travel. . . .

Until one snowy day in the wilds of North Dakota, when Duke, still in his blue bathrobe at two in the afternoon, announced to no one in particular: "I think I'll bring you expensive gentlemen (and one ultra-expensive lady) to Europe this spring."

Eight

"Ain't she a beaut!" whistled Rabbit as we stood by the Hudson River docks. For once he wasn't talking about a girl. In front of us, towering at least ten stories high, stood the ocean liner *Champlain*. It was March 23, 1939, and an icy drizzle was pelting down.

Ivie didn't look so sure. "Didn't the *Titanic* also have four smoke stacks?" she asked.

"Why, yes, it did," said Sonny, his eyes bulging and his face deadpan, "and I think the *Lusitania* had four as well."

Poor Ivie looked green.

Soon Duke, driven by Mercer and accompanied by Ruth and Jonesy, arrived. Grunting, Jonesy and I hauled the maestro's seven trunks on board and into his stateroom. *Why seven?* you may ask. Well, the man loved his custom-tailored suits; his dozens of silk shirts; and his pair after pair of soft, custom-made

shoes. Although he could get as "down home" as anyone, Duke Ellington loved his luxury.

"Where am I sleeping?" I asked Jonesey.

"Actually, Duke nabbed you a nice room—small,
but nice."

He wasn't kidding. It was a cozy room, really a
closet, three flights below deck, with a bed, a dresser,
a tiny bathroom, and, best of all, a porthole. Opening
it, all I could see was a wall of black—the ship in the
next berth—but I knew that soon, very soon, I'd be
looking out over the Atlantic Ocean. I laid my satchel
and my trumpet on my bed. There was a knock; it was
Rabbit.

"Not bad, kid, not bad," he said, looking around.

"I can't believe that I'm going to see London and
Paris and all these other places," I said.

He sat down on my bed. This was unusual for Rabbit—he was not often in the mood to talk. "I hear
you. I joined Duke in 1928, right out of Beantown.
You see, both Harry and I knew each other as kids
in Boston and he was the one who convinced me to
join this band. 'Duke's going places,' he said—and he
wasn't kidding!"

"You've been to Europe before, right?"

"Yeah, in '33. You're not going to believe it—the
people over there are so crazy for jazz that they actually
know the catalog numbers of our recordings! I'll never

forget this French kid saying, 'On July 25, 1928, you played on *Yellow Dog Blues* on the Okeh label, number 8602. Was this your first recording session for Duke?' My mouth must've fell a mile. Just get ready—they're *fanatics* over there."

"Was the kid right?" I asked.

"Right about what?"

"*Was* that your first session for Duke?"

Rabbit smiled sheepishly. "Yeah. The kid was right—although I'd forgotten the date. I just knew that it was the summer of '28. Hey, listen, Dan—I've been meaning to tell you. . . ." For a second I grew nervous. You never knew if Rabbit was pulling your leg. "Your trumpet playing has been really improving lately. I heard you practicing backstage in Cincinnati last week. You have a real sweet sound with plenty of soul. Just keep on playing and, who knows, Duke might find a place for you in our band."

Man, those words shot me to the top of the world. Rabbit never complimented *anyone*, rarely even smiled. "Thanks, Rab," I said.

"I speak the truth, kid. Hey, come up on deck soon. Pulling out of the harbor is a sight you'll never forget."

He was right. It was a chilly, breezy March afternoon, and the Hudson River and New York Harbor were a jumble of whitecaps, with seagulls riding the air currents above us. As we passed the Statue of Liberty, I thought back to my first visit with Harry and Rex almost two years before. I'd seen a huge chunk of the United States since then, and now I was on my way to Europe! As our ship glided out into the open Atlantic, leaving the gray skyscrapers behind, old bald Barney shivered, saying, "I'll feel a whole lot better when I see that statue the next time."

"Why?" I asked.

Barney didn't suffer fools. "Don't you read the newspapers, kid? The Germans and the Italians are gearing up for another world war. Man, we've barely recovered from the first one. And Hitler and his Nazis despise black folks and jazz. Nigger music, they charmingly call it." For a second that word had me back in Georgia, hearing white boys in dirty overalls calling me that as I shopped for Granny in our local store.

"Are we going to Germany?" I asked.

"No," replied Barney, "they don't want us—and that's fine with me."

In no time, Long Island was just a speck on the horizon, and then nothing at all, and we were truly out at sea.

Nine

"What is *wrong* with that kid?" groaned Sonny, as I dug into my third helping of pancakes. I'd slept soundly in my cozy bunk; naturally I was now famished.

"Hey, I'm a growing boy."

Poor Sonny's face was as green as an Irish golf course. "Um, excuse me," he said, rushing out of the breakfast restaurant.

With the exception of us, all the rest of the passengers were white, but they were friendly enough. "Hey, Duke, how come you don't dance like Cab Calloway?" some fat dude in a loud sports coat asked.

Without a pause, his fork still held aloft, Duke replied, "My *confrere* Monsieur Calloway has that avocation so well covered—and with such *élan*—that I wouldn't dare infringe on his territory."

The fat guy looked confused, sputtered out a "yeah, right," and returned to his sausages.

Man, Duke could be smooth! Yet he could also be distant and dreamy. During our voyage he mostly sat by himself in a deck chair, wrapped up snug against the cold, humming and composing—always composing. You rarely ever saw the man without pencil and paper nearby. Both Ruth and Mercer had stayed behind in Sugar Hill, so there were no family members he had to worry about. "Daniel," he said to me one morning, "my life consists of travel and dreaming." Twirling his pencil, he smiled. "*Composing* is just a fancy word for dreaming. I'm always dreaming up some music or another and scratching it down before it vanishes." He smiled. "What a life. . . ."

A few times, however, Duke left his musical dreams behind and joined the rest of us mortals in the floating poker games that were always going on, dawn to dusk and straight through to dawn again. I'd become quite the player myself, with a poker face to match Tricky Sam's. "What are you going to *do* with all that loot?" Barney asked as I raked in yet another hefty pot.

"Give it to your mother," I replied. "I heard she spent three hours at the beauty parlor the other day— and that was just for an estimate!"

The table roared, Rabbit nodded in approval—(for he had coached me)—and I felt such approval, such acceptance from these people I so admired, that all these years later my chest still swells with pride.

Being at sea also gave me plenty of time to practice my trumpet. Under Rex and Cootie's tutelage, I was building up a strong, muscular *embouchure* (musician talk for lips and mouth), and I found that some of the music I could imagine I could also translate through my horn.

"You're getting there, Daniel," said Rex one windy afternoon, the ocean reflecting the sunlight in every direction. "I'll never forget the day when I realized that I was no longer playing the trumpet—that I was playing *myself*. It was my *own* thoughts and emotions pouring out of my horn. For a guy who's only been playing for two years, you're really coming along."

"Do you think Duke will let me join his orchestra one day?"

Rex thought for a moment. "Hmm . . . now that's a tough one. On the one hand, the Gov'nor values individual expression, but on the other he has exact standards." He could see my expression. "Hey, just keep on practicing and playing and playing and practicing and one of these days you might be snatching a job right out from under . . . Cootie!"

On the deck above us stood Jimmy, wrapped in a camel's hair coat and a red scarf, his bass beside him, playing into the wind. His ever-present cough couldn't be heard, but I knew it was there. "Now look at that kid," said Rex. "He's considered the finest bassist in all of jazz—he has pros *twice* his age studying his technique—but he's *still* relentless in his practicing. The people who pay to dance to our music don't understand the dedication and skill it takes to play our music."

I thought about what I wanted to say. I didn't want to sound foolish. "When I'm really into playing my horn, I feel like I'm daydreaming out loud. That I'm putting my deepest thoughts into music. I don't know if that makes sense or not, but—"

Suddenly Rex had me in a bear hug. "That's *good*, Daniel! In fact, that's *great!* That's how I feel, too, when I'm really into the music. You've perfectly expressed what I've always felt: *Daydreaming out loud.* You're quite the philosopher, my friend." Stepping back, he snatched a piece of lint off my coat. "Now let's go do something worthwhile—like eat!"

• • • •

Most nights, after a few hours of poker and chat, I'd turn in around midnight. Often, though, I'd toss and turn in my little bed, with one thought shooting across my mind: *The Atlantic Ocean is out there—don't waste it!* So I'd dress and climb up the stairs to the deck, stand at the railing, and look out at the sea. One night a trail of moonlight, liquid and shimmery, ran to the edge of the world. On other nights the stars seemed close enough to touch. And on another night it drizzled, the smell of the rain mingling with the thick ocean smell. Every night was bone-biting cold, often with a slicing, wet wind, but Ivie had bought me a warm brown camel's hair coat. I'd stand at the railing, wondering how deep was the water, if we were sailing over drowned folks' bones and sunken ships, if we were passing over whales and sharks. One cloudy night I heard something splash out of the water and land with a *smack*, but I couldn't see what it was. *It's March, 1939*, I'd tell myself. *You're with Duke sailing across the Atlantic. Remember how this feels!*

"You're up late," said a voice one night, startling me. It belonged to Juan, one of Duke's three trombonists. Tricky Sam was a pal, always giving me poker tips and telling stories of the West Indies. But the other two, Lawrence and Juan, kept to themselves. Tall and serious, Lawrence seemed like a minister and would only greet me with a nod. Since I'd heard that Juan had a temper and carried a knife, I never got in his way. A light-skinned man, he had once darkened his face with make-up when we played a dance in Texas.

"I figure this trip will be over in no time," I said, "so I might as well experience every second."

Juan laughed softly. "Some people—precious few—live their lives that way." He looked out over the darkened water. "It's all over too quickly."

We stood there, silently, for at least ten minutes before Juan said, "Good night" and left the deck.

The next morning I was late for breakfast. The waiters were cleaning up the egg and syrup stained dishes. At a corner table, writing furiously in his calf-skin journal, sat Rex. As I sat down next to him, he scribbled on. Finally, when a waiter waltzed over to take my order, Rex looked up.

"I'm sorry, Daniel, I didn't even know you were there."

"No problem. What're you writing?"

Closing the journal, he smiled sadly. "I try to write portraits of the musicians I know and have known. Right now I'm writing about Jimmy Harrison, an old friend of mine who died young."

"Did he play with Duke?" I asked.

"Briefly—but long before I joined the band. No, Jimmy made his mark with the Fletcher Henderson band. He was one of the finest trombonists I've ever heard. Ask Tricky Sam about him some time—he still gets tears in his eyes about old Jimmy."

"What did he die of?"

"Stomach cancer—about eight years ago. Man, he was one sharp-dressed cat and when he walked down 135th Street the ladies would *snap* to attention. He never went to college but he was reading all the time and could tell you stuff about math and Persia and how many bases Ty Cobb stole in 1919."

I took a sip of the coffee the waiter had just poured.

"So what do you write *about?*" I asked.

Rex smiled. "I got the idea from Duke, to tell you the truth. The Gov'nor, as you know, writes *musical* portraits of people, so I figured that I can write *word* portraits about some of the folks *I've* known." He sipped at his coffee. "You know, writing is a great deal like playing music. When I'm playing my horn I'm trying to tell a story by choosing the right notes with which to *tell* that story. And writing's the same—only now I'm searching for the right *words* to describe my friends." He closed up his journal. "Next up— Duke—although describing someone as mercurial as that man will be difficult."

By now my breakfast had arrived and I was digging in for all I was worth. "Mercurial?"

Rex's broad face broke into another smile. He liked people as curious as he was. "Changeable—like the mercury on a thermometer. Hey, you up for a morning music lesson?"

Of course I was.

Ten

Duke squeezed the back of my neck. "I do believe, Daniel, that that's France up ahead."

It was March 30, an exact week since the *Champlain* had sailed out of New York Harbor. Up ahead a line of green seemed to be peeping up out of the sea.

Otto, an outgoing musician who strangely never had much to say to me, whistled. "Just think of all of those French ladies a-waitin' on Otto."

Sonny gave him a good-natured elbow to the ribs. "Yeah, a-waitin' on Otto to buy them a drink—before they leave the joint with old Sonny!"

Ivie shot them both a look that said, *There's a child present*, (a look which, by the way, I hated), and wrapped an arm around me. "You're going to love Paris, Danny—the most beautiful city I've ever seen."

"Is that Paris up ahead?" I asked.

"No," said Duke, "that's Le Havre. We'll then take

a train to Paris. Wait a minute. . . . Am I losing my mind or do I hear music?"

Those of us at the railing all strained our ears and, sure enough, the sound of ragtimey jazz was being carried over the waves. At first the music was indistinct, a blur, but then Jonesy said, "Hey! It's *It Don't Mean A Thing*!"

Producing a pair of binoculars from out of nowhere, Sonny said, "Folks, there's hundreds of 'em, dancing, jumping, holding up hot club signs. Man, Le Havre is going nuts!"

"What's a *hot club*?" I asked.

"European jazz fans form these clubs," said Otto, "and they meet to listen to records and discuss jazz. Some hot clubs even have their own bands. You should hear the Quintet of the Hot Club of France. They have this gypsy guitar player, Django Reinhardt, who's sensational."

"He'd be a fine addition to our band," murmured Duke, his eyes scanning the ever-approaching shore. "Hey, Sonny's right for once—they *do* have signs!"

Welcome, Duke! read one sign. *Ellington forever!* The white shops and homes of Le Havre were now growing more distinct; I could see a mob of French folks, mostly young, gathered along the docks. Many were dancing to the band, which was now playing *I Let a Song Go Out of My Heart*, one of my favorites.

79

Within an hour, we were stepping off the gang-plank into the crowd, which swarmed around us. Since I was carrying my satchel in one hand and my trumpet in another, the people assumed that I was also a member of the band. Many in the crowd were carrying their own instruments, showing that they too were musicians. It was crazy. Everywhere folks were shouting and dancing and calling out various names: *"Doook!" "Coo-tee!" "Raa-beet!" "Har-ree!" "Eye-vee!" "Jim-mee!" "Rex!"* The band, a five piece, quite good, had kicked it up a notch. Suddenly, Duke was hoisted onto the shoulders of several young men and he, along with the rest of us, was escorted to the Le Havre train station.

A half hour later, on the now speeding train, Duke rushed up and down the dining-car aisle, say-ing, "Wasn't that incredible? Ivie, I saw your delicate bloomers when those lads picked you up! Purple, eh? Rab, do you see why I pay you so extravagantly?" (To which Rabbit simply rolled his eyes).

I was sitting next to Rex, a hot meal before us. Duke noticed that my friend had tears in his eyes. "What gives, Fat Stuff?" he asked.

It took a moment for Rex to collect himself. "I don't know, Duke. It was just . . . back home we have gas station attendants telling us that we can't use the rest rooms, but here. . . . For the first time in my life

I had the feeling of being accepted as an artist, a gentleman, and a member of the human race."

Now Duke wasn't one to show emotion—*keep cool at all moments* was his creed—but his eyes, too, were moist. "I know what you mean, friend, I know what you mean." I kept my mouth shut, but I wondered if Duke was recalling the words of that red-faced cop back in Washington: "Duke, if you'd been born a white man, you'd've been one great musician." What a fool.

In a flash that sardonic smile was back on Duke's face. "Hey, Fat Stuff, even though the jury's still out on whether or not you're a gentleman, I've *always* known that you are an artist of the first rank." Squeezing Rex's shoulder, Duke moved on down the dining car.

We pulled into Paris' Gare du Nord, where another friendly mob had gathered to greet us. After a brief press conference in which Duke smiled and spoke his convoluted high-talk, several taxis delivered us to our small, homey hotel on the rue de l'Harpe, and Rex and I, roomies once again, fell instantly asleep.

And now, reader, you're all caught up.

Eleven

Harry's face beamed with pride. "Do you know that we're playing only *concerts* on this tour? No high school prom dances, no Alabama barns with chicken wire to protect us. *Concerts* in Paris, Brussels, Antwerp, The Hague, Amsterdam, then onto Sweden and Norway! Can you believe this?"

It was evening in the dressing room of the spanking new National Theatre de Chaillot, just across from the Eiffel Tower. Jonesy bounced in, breathless. "The stage manager says that there's over 2,800 folks out there. It's crazy!"

Everyone was so excitedly tense that, after setting up Sonny's drums, I simply felt in the way. Sneaking out of the theater, I walked out into the night. A misty rain was falling over Paris and there, across the river, stood the Eiffel Tower, all lit up in golds and greens. Hustling down several flights of stairs, I hightailed it across a bridge and was soon standing beneath the tower. Looking up, I felt like I was standing beneath the legs of a sleeping iron giant. At any moment it could awaken and trample me to bits. For a country boy from Georgia, who had seen pictures of Paris in his geography book at school, this was a big moment, don't you doubt that!

It was soon dark. Hungry, I decided to look for a restaurant. Walking down narrow, cobblestoned streets, slick and glistening in the rain, I passed bakery after bakery, café after café. In each one, couples seemed warm and cozy and happy, drinking wine, eating food, chatting. The rain had picked up, so I ducked into a dark, smoky smelling café. A waiter asked me something in French, I said *oui*, and he led me to a small table by the window. Now Rex had taught me how to say several dishes in French, but with the waiter standing over me I only remembered one—*omelette du jambon*, ham omelette—which sounded fine. The people around me were drinking wine, either red or white, but I knew I was too young for that, so I said, "Milk, please" to the waiter. He looked at me as if I'd just spoken gibberish, so I said it again: "Milk, please." Again, that befuddled look. Now after saying the word *milk* my entire life and having folks understand me, it was very strange to have this dude looking so perplexed. Thinking quick, I pantomimed the milking of a cow's udder (which I had seen done quite often back home), and let out a deep, guttural, "*Mooooo!*"

Nodding abruptly, the waiter turned and walked to the kitchen. Quite satisfied with my method of communication, I sat back and waited for my meal (and milk) to arrive. I didn't have long to wait. "*Va!*" yelled a tall *garcon* with a mustache. "*Va maintenant!*"

"I don't understand," I said.

"*Va! Maintenant!*"

An old man sitting over a coffee leaned over. "He's asking you to go—right now," he explained in accented English.

"But why?"

"He thinks you were rude with your cow milking. I thought it was quite clever myself." He dropped a few coins on his table. "Here, let's go before he grows even uglier."

I now found myself standing on the drizzly sidewalk beside a chuckling old man. "Forgive me for finding it funny," he said, "but it was. My name is Henri."

"I'm Danny," I said. "I'm not from here."

Again, the old man chuckled. His eyes were watery and very blue. "*Oui, je sais.* I know. Right across the street is another café where we can order you your ham omelette and a glass of milk. Agreed?"

Now I know all about not talking to strangers and

all, but he was a very slight old man, and I could have outrun him without even trying. So I agreed. In a few moments he had ordered my meal and another coffee for himself in a cozy café with a guitarist playing softly by a fireplace.

"So, Dan-nee, where are you from?" he asked.

"Georgia—in the United States. I'm here with Duke Ellington's Orchestra. They're playing right now at the Theatre de Chaillot."

Henri's eyes widened. "*Oui*, I know that too. All of Paris has been very excited about this concert. Tickets are very hard to obtain. He's an exceptional composer, your Duke."

"Thanks," I said stupidly, as if I had anything to do with Duke's never-ending creativity.

"But aren't you afraid?" he asked.

My omelette (and milk) had arrived and I was digging in. "Of what?"

"The Nazis."

"But they're in Germany."

Henri's blue eyes looked very sad. "But they could start a war at any time—and they hate black folks as well as us Jews. If a war were to break out while you were here, you'd be in danger."

I swallowed my food. "But you don't think there's going to be a war, do you?" I recalled Barney's words as we'd sailed past the Statue of Liberty.

The old man nodded. "Oh, yes, war is certain. Adolf Hitler wants war and he will get it. The only question is when. Since I'm Jewish, I've tried to emigrate to your country, but only a few people are being allowed in."

"Why?" I couldn't see why the United States was not allowing such a kind old man to enter. I could think of a few white bigots that the government could swap him for.

With a wave of his hand, he said, "Oh, I don't blame your country. You've suffered under your Depression and so many Americans are out of work that it doesn't make sense to allow more workers in. But I worry. . . ."

Now Rex had told me that in a week we'd be crossing through northern Germany on our way from Holland to Denmark. Duke had tried to seek permission to play in Hamburg and Berlin, both German cities, but had been told in a telegram that the government didn't condone *nigger music*. "My, and I thought we played jazz," Duke had said.

When I told this to Henri, he said, "My advice? Don't stop too long. Yet I can't see the Nazis harming the world famous Duke Ellington. The outcry would be tremendous. By the way, what is he like?"

Draining the last of my milk—*lait du froid*, it was called in French—I thought for a moment. "Hmm . . .

well, he's as friendly as all get out, and he doesn't seem to have a stuck-up bone in his body. In all the dancehalls we play in America, Duke knows all the custodians by name, and after a show you can find him with them rolling dice, and if he wins he gives them the money (with plenty more added) before he leaves. But . . . there's something distant about him. He can really duck back into his head, and his eyes get this distant look, and you know then not to bother him."

Henri laughed. "Just as I thought—he's a true artist. Beethoven was the same—but without the friendliness and lack of ego."

I insisted on paying for Henri's coffee and he let me, but I had a reason. As we stood outside the café, I said, "To tell you the truth, Henri, I have no idea how to get back to the theater. The rain's let up a little. Could you please show me the way back?"

Of course, this was no trouble for this kind old man. We said goodbye by the stage door. "Would you like to come in to hear the show?" I asked. "I can get you in for free."

He shook my hand. "No, no, but I thank you for your offer. My wife sent me out hours ago to buy some pastry, and if I'm not home soon I will be in for it. But thank you, Danny. It was a pleasure to meet you, son. *Au revoir.*"

In the many years since, knowing what happened to France (and France's Jewish folks) under the Nazis, I've often wondered what became of this kind, blue-eyed old man. Sadly, I can guess.

• • • •

The show was in full swing as I entered back stage. Picking up my trumpet, I stood by the plush purple curtains and played softly along with the band. *The Black and Tan Fantasy . . . Old King Dooji . . .* Rex's specialty *Boy Meets Horn . . . Mood Indigo . . . Creole Love Call . . . Blue Ramble . . . Dusk in the Desert . . . It Don't Mean a Thing . . . Solitude . . . I Let a Song Go Out of My Heart. . . .* Duke and his men played for hours, and the French people went nuts. Yet when Harry stepped forward with his big baritone sax to play *Prelude to a Kiss*, the theater was as quiet as a church at midnight. Then Rabbit stepped to the microphone to play *Jeep's Blues* and we were back in a rowdy roadhouse.

The applause at show's end continued for at least twenty minutes. The band played encore after encore. Duke would've played some more, but an official looking dude said that it would violate a curfew law.

My eyes were bugging out at all of the gorgeous French women who flocked backstage to meet Duke. He was full of his flattery, telling one lady (who didn't deserve the compliment, by the way), "My, you make that dress look lovely." Another lady leaned low and kissed me on the cheek!

As Rex, Tricky Sam, Harry and I walked back to our hotel, people everywhere tipped their hats or said the French version of *Howdy* to us. For some reason the four of us were quiet as we passed the crowded cafes and the dark, shut-up bakeries. The rain had stopped and the stars were bright over Paris and I don't think I've ever known so perfect a moment.

Twelve

The next morning Rex and Barney brought me to a hill in the north of Paris called Montmartre. The clouds above the city floated past like lazy white whales, and it was cool in the shadows. In an open square full of painters and their easels, we ate breakfast at an outdoor café. I couldn't believe how delicious a simple meal of bread, jam, and *cafe au lait* could be.

Rex, who could read French better than he could speak it, was slowly translating our reviews from the morning newspapers. "Let's see," he said, holding a paper called *Le Figaro*. "'*By what orchestral imagination . . . does one arrive at these strange . . . fluted . . . sound effects . . . atmospheric vibrations with powerful humor.' Hmm,* I *think* that's what it says."

Through a mouthful of bread, Barney asked, "But what does that *mean?*"

"Beats me," said Rex. "Wait, here's another: '*Such music is not only a new art form but a new reason for living.*' Yikes!"

"Yeah, let's cut that one out and show it to the next white restaurant manager who won't let us eat in his joint," Barney said with some bitterness.

"Or a city hotel that won't take us," added Rex.

I wondered why I didn't feel as bitter. I didn't mind staying on the train, or sometimes sleeping in the rooming houses in the black part of town, or eating in the restaurants labeled *Colored Served In Back*. The sheets and towels were clean and the food was always hot and good. I figured it was because the band hadn't always had the train—and because I was so young and just glad to be part of a family, seeing the world. Besides, Duke was always footing the bill for me. To be fair, Rex and Barney had been doing more than their share of traveling for more years than I'd been alive.

I must have been rather dim that morning because something suddenly occurred to me. "Hey, why'd you two bring your instruments?"

Rex swallowed his last piece of bread. "Because we have a recording session this morning. You're welcome to come along if you wish."

The studio was within walking distance. We passed by the huge white dome of Sacre Coeur church, overlooking all of Paris. In the distance I could see Notre

Dame, the River Seine, and my misty friend from the night before, the Eiffel Tower.

An intense-eyed, mustachioed man was already in the studio, seated on a stool, hunched over a guitar, strumming the most rhythmic, complex lines I'd ever heard. Looking up, he muttered, *Bon matin*, and returned to his guitar.

"Django doesn't know much English," explained Barney, "so don't try to talk his ear off. I've heard that he can't read or write either."

I noticed that the man's left hand, his fretting hand, was misshapen, with a star-like explosion of skin shooting from its center. His two smallest fingers seemed fused together. "What's up with his hand?" I whispered.

Barney cupped his hand over my ear. "He's a gypsy. They travel around in their wagons, which they call *roulottes*. About ten years ago a fire broke out in Django's *roulotte*. While saving his mother's life, his hand was horribly burned. Everyone thought that that was the end of his career as a guitarist, but he simply learned a new way to play." Barney beamed. "Listen—he's magnificent."

Magnificent was just the word to describe Django Reinhardt's music. Fluid lines of graceful, rhythmic notes and strummed chords poured from his battered guitar. Hunched over on his stool, he seemed lost in another world.

"Are you capturing this?" Rex asked the recording engineer, who was behind a glass wall. The man cupped an ear to show that he hadn't heard the question.

After glorious minutes of spinning out his incredible music, seemingly out of midair, Django signaled that he was ready. By this time Jimmy, looking ragged out and, as always, coughing, had arrived by taxi with his bass. "Sorry I'm late," he panted, "but I fell into the most amazing jam session last night—and it just ended."

Clucking his tongue like a concerned mother, Rex said, "Right after this session, Jim, you're heading back to the hotel and *sleeping*. Understand?"

Jimmy nodded. "Any food here?"

There wasn't, but there *were* five songs to record. Speaking through a microphone to the engineer, who understood English, Rex said, "This one's called *Montmartre (Django's Jump)*." Picking up his clarinet, Barney joined Rex's cornet and Jimmy's bass and they ran through the song several times, while Django silently watched and listened, pungent tobacco smoke encircling his head. On the fourth go-round, the gypsy nodded, picked up his guitar, and played counterpoint lines to Rex's tune as though he'd known it his entire life. It was a perfect take.

"Too bad that wasn't recorded," said Barney. From

attending several of Duke's recording sessions in New York, I knew that the recording gear was rolling when the red light on the wall was fired up.

"But it was," said the engineer through his microphone. "Our red light is broken."

The four other numbers were handled the same way—Duke's musicians running through the "changes" for Django, who smoked cigarette after cigarette, listening intently. Then he'd pick up his well-traveled guitar and simply play magic.

Django said nothing to me, but when the session was over he winked and shook my hand. (I tried not to squeeze too hard). Rex offered him a ticket to that night's show at the Theatre de Chaillot, (while the engineer handed him a fistful of French francs), but to the best of my knowledge, Django didn't go.

Afterwards, Rex, Barney and I stood on the sidewalk outside of the studio. Jimmy, despite his promise, had hailed a cab and was off with his bass to yet another jam session.

"I'm just going to walk around for a while, guys," I said. (Was it my imagination that both of my friends seemed relieved?)

"Now look *both ways* before you cross the streets," warned Rex, "and be at the theater by five bells."

"What are you two up to?" I asked.

Barney wagged a finger at me. "Look both ways

before you cross *any* street, lad," and away they sauntered.

Speaking of sauntering, I did a bit of it myself as I strolled down the steep hill of Montmartre. The sun was bright and the air smelled of bread and bus diesel. In the Place Pigalle a small record shop was blasting Duke's *Braggin' in Brass*, recorded the year before, so naturally I sauntered right in. I was browsing through the jazz 78s—thick slabs of black shellac—when a female voice said something to me in French.

"I'm sorry, I don't understand," I said to a girl a few years older than I. She had saucy brown eyes, coffee-colored skin, and a spray of black curls.

"Oh, you're a Yankee!" she said in heavily accented English. When I giggled, her brown eyes flashed and she demanded, "What's so funny? I said it right."

"Nothing. I'm sorry. I've just never heard a black girl speak with a French accent before, that's all."

She tossed those curls. Man, her hair smelled like flowers. "That's because I was born in Par-ee, Simple Simon. My father is from Rhodesia and my mama's French." She stuck out her hand. "I'm Chanel."

"I'm Dan. I'm from Georgia, but now I'm living in Harlem with Duke Ellington and his sister."

She looked me up and down. "Funny, you don't *look* like a liar."

To heck with her, I thought, and began browsing

95

through the Count Basie section. "If you don't believe me, come to the stage door of the Theatre de Chaillot tonight at eight. Ask for Dan. I'll be there."

Slapping me on the back, she said, "You *are* telling the truth! Follow me, Dan-nee the Yank."

Since Chanel's walk was a trot, I had to hustle to keep up. Dashing out the door of the shop, she turned a corner into an alley. A red motorbike was leaning against a brick wall. "Fancy a tour of Par-ee?" she asked.

"Sure. I just have to be at the theater by five."

"Plenty of time. Hop on!" I climbed on behind her. "Once we get rolling, Dan-nee the Yank, you're going to have to wrap your arms around me. Don't be shy. I don't bite."

Soon her motorbike was whizzing down the Rue de Rivoli, weaving in and out of the plodding traffic. Chanel's delicious hair tickled my face as she chatted away, describing the sights. *I'm in Paris, France. The sun's shining and I have my arms wrapped around a pretty girl's waist. Man, the life of a traveling cymbal shiner!*

• • • •

From the swirling Place de la Concorde to the bustling Champs Elysees; from the leafy Jardin de Tuileries to the leafy Jardin de Luxembourg; from the wide boulevards of the Right Bank to the bumpy cobblestones of the Left Bank—I saw it all from the back of Chanel's red motorbike.

For a spell we took a breather on a bench beside the River Seine. The good citizens of Paris strolled past and quite a few were kissing.

"So, what do Yankee boys do for fun?"

"Back home in Georgia I'd go fishing a lot, but now that I'm traveling with Duke . . . well . . . I guess you could say that almost every moment of every day is fun."

She brushed away several lovely curls from her eyes. "Why?"

"Because every day is different—different towns, different cities. Pretty soon it's going to be different countries. My life is always changing. What do *you* do for fun?"

Her brown eyes were watching a barge glide beneath a bridge. "Oh, just what we're doing. When I'm not in school I'm riding my motorbike through Paris, enjoying the city, and talking to people. My papa works on a barge like that one there and some days he takes me to work with him. I love that. Almost every night my parents go out and I stay in and watch my little brother."

In a few moments we were back on the bike and *la Tour Eiffel* loomed up ahead. "There's the theater," I said. "You can leave me off right over there."

Reluctantly unlocking my arms, I stepped off the motorbike. "I can leave tickets for you and your parents for tonight's show," I said. I wouldn't have minded a nighttime ride through Paris with old Chanel.

"Who'd watch my brother?" she asked.

"I'll leave a ticket for him, too."

"He's two. No, thank you, Dan-ee the Yank—but thank you for a wonderful afternoon." Leaning over, she kissed me on the cheek. "You're very cute. Too bad you're a traveling man."

And with a roaring *put-put* Chanel was gone.

Thirteen

That second show in Paris was as well-attended and well-received as the first. "We love you madly!" Duke called to the crowd after yet another series of encores. This night, however, we all had to hustle to reach a station called the Gare d'Orsay to catch the midnight train to Belgium, a country I'd never even *heard* of before. After working like a young horse to help Jonesy load up all of the band's instruments, lights, and sound equipment, I fell instantly asleep in my berth.

In the morning, about an hour away from Brussels, I sat in the dining car next to Cootie, both of us digging into our plates of ham and eggs.

"So she just asked you to hop on her motorbike?" he asked, a bit of egg falling from his mouth.

"Yup—it was great. I had my arms around her waist and, man, her hair smelled *so good*."

Washing down his food with a swig of coffee, Cootie's smile lit up the dining car. "My man!"

I smiled, too. "Yeah, but the only thing, Coots, is that I sort of *miss* her now. Hanging out with her just made me want to hang out with her some more."

The trumpeter nodded sadly. "The curse of the road, Daniel, the curse of the road." For a while we ate in silence, then Cootie said, "You and Rex sure like reading them books."

"Rex says since I'm not going to school that I should be reading all the time."

"What kind of stuff do you two read?"

"For a while Rex had me reading histories about Africa and how our people were brought over as slaves," I said. "Now he has me plowing through the novels of Charles Dickens. I didn't like *Bleak House* too much—too bleak—but I really enjoyed *Great Expectations* and *David Copperfield.*"

Cootie sipped his coffee. "Hmm . . . my granddaddy was a slave. Used to tell me stories of how he was sold away from his parents when he was only eight years old. 'I can still hear my mama's screams in my memory,' he'd say." Cootie shook his head. "I just can't imagine."

I didn't mention it, but every once in a while Granny would wake up in the dead of night shrieking. I learned to simply ignore it and fall back to sleep, but she once explained to me: "Those are my memory-dreams of the time when my brother and two older sisters were sold away from our parents. No one told us where they were going—they were just hauled off like cattle. I was only four and allowed to stay, but my brother was only seven and my sisters were eight year old twin girls. In my dreams it's all happening again."

"Did you ever see them again, Granny?" I had asked.

"My brother, yes—after the war was ended—but my two sisters died of some illness not long after being sold." She had gazed out our cabin window at the falling rain. "I can still see their little faces in my mind. . . ."

My daydream was interrupted by Rabbit saying, "Hey, scoot over, Dan." After ordering his breakfast, he said, "We should be in Brussels soon. *Man!* Look at that!" He pointed out the window. All I saw were green fields sprinkled with yellow flowers and haystacks.

"What're you pointing at, Rab?" asked Cootie.

"Look closely at those haystacks—there's men in them."

Barney, seated behind us, had put on his glasses. "You're right. They're all putting something into those haystacks. I'm sorry—they're just whizzing by too fast to see."

"They're machine guns," said Harry's deep voice. "Those men are placing machine gun posts in all of those haystacks. Look at those ditches out yonder. They're putting guns in those, too."

"But why?" asked a voice—I believe it was Otto's.

"Because there could be a war coming," said another voice—Duke's. He sat down. "Good morning, folks. Wonderful show last night." The dining car was quiet as we all watched the Belgium men preparing their homeland for possible war. "I've been wondering the past few days if I should've brought you all here."

"Ah, don't worry, Gov-nor," said Rex, "we've got a secret weapon—Ivie. Those Nazis don't know what they're up against if they go up against *that* woman!"

"Only in poker, Fat Stuff," said the lady herself, who had quietly entered the dining car, looking fresh and pretty in a yellow dress. Punching me on the shoulder, she scooted next to me. "Other than in a poker game, I come in peace."

"Or when you're punching people," I added.

Duke was already digging into his second helping of eggs and steak. "Ivie, dear," he said between mouthfuls, "I've worked up a new arrangement of *Rose of the Rio Grande*. Let's work on it after breakfast."

"Sure, Duke," she said. Now she shot an elbow into my sides. *Are you going to ask him?* her eyes clearly said.

Ask who what? my eyes tried to answer.

"Duke," she said, clearing her throat. The maestro looked up from his meal. "Daniel here has been working hard on several trumpet obbligatos for *Rose*, and I have to say that they're sounding quite tasty. How about taking a listen?"

"Sure, sure—but he's not playing on stage with us here. A midnight dance in Paducah, Kentucky is fine, but not Europe. You've come a long way, Daniel, but you're not quite there yet."

This conversation embarrassed me. I'd never asked Ivie to joust on my behalf. To be honest, I was facing reality and losing the fire to play onstage. Although I practiced my horn daily under the tutelage of Rex and Cootie (and enjoyed playing), I had no illusions of being the next Rex Stewart or Cootie Williams. I was evolving into a solid player—but I was no phenom. "No problem, Duke," I said. "I don't feel like I'm ready yet either."

Sticking out her tongue at me, Ivie turned to the window and gazed out. "Hey, there's men out there putting machine guns in those haystacks. . . ."

Our hotel in Brussels was on a quiet, leafy street, close to Leopold Park. "Our concert is at the *Palais de Beaux Arts* at eight," said Duke in the lobby. "I want everyone there by five. Hop into any taxi and the driver will take you there."

"Pa-lay duh bowz arts," said Tricky Sam. "Man, if I don't repeat these foreign names out loud then I forget 'em. Hey, have you finished my book yet, Dan?"

He had loaned me a book on the black leader Marcus Garvey and his Back to Africa Movement. Although I liked old Marcus, I had no interest in moving to Africa. As far as I could tell, Tricky wasn't going to make the big move anytime soon either.

"I'm almost done, Trick," I said, itching to go upstairs, throw down my satchel, grab a quick shower, and hit the streets.

"I'm going to take a walk," I said to Rex after my shower. "Want to come along?" My friend's rhythmic snoring gave me his answer.

It was a raw, cloudy day, threatening rain, but the weather went along perfectly with the narrow, cobblestoned streets, chocolate shops, churches, and cafés of Brussels. From the shops I could hear French being spoken, but also another language that I took to be Dutch. After stopping into a shadowy, incense-scented church to say a quick prayer for Granny, I stopped for a cup of coffee at a café.

"What's a personage of your shade doing in these parts?" asked a gruff voice from behind a newspaper.

"Minding my own," I replied.

The newspaper dropped. It was Duke! "Sit down, Daniel," he said, his eyes laughing. "*Garcon? A café au lait* for *mon ami*." I saw that his table was filled with musical notation paper, scribbled with notes that I could not read. The newspaper had been a momentary break.

"But you're busy," I said. "I don't want to bother you."

"Nonsense. You and I never grab a moment to gab." Now this was the thing about Duke Ellington: he was tall and very good-looking; he seemed to know beautiful ladies in every town and city we visited; he was world-famous; Rex showed me articles that European scholars and even classical composers were writing about his work. Yet . . . he never made you feel that he was above you. He always made you feel as if *you* were important, too. Although he was always putting people on, I think he honestly felt that he was no better than anyone else.

"But you're always so busy," I said, "and I'm just a kid."

He thanked the waiter, who had just brought our coffees. "So what? I was a kid once—I wasn't always the empty husk of a man that you see today before you."

I laughed—Duke always made me laugh. "What's it like?" I asked.

"What's what like?"

"To be so creative—to always be creating something that people love."

Smiling, Duke looked out the window. "It's wonderful, Danny, it really is. I began playing piano when I was about your age for just one reason—it made the little fillies stand by my elbow at parties. Then I wrote my first song—*Soda Fountain Rag*, I called it—and it just rolled out of me. Now I can't stop—I'm even composing when I sleep. I can't tell you how many times I've woken up with a tune in my head. That's why I keep my notebooks and pencils right by my bed. And *that's* why I keep my band on the road—so that when I compose a piece of music, I can hear it played by fine musicians the very next day, sometimes in the very same *hour* as I wrote it! Just think—there are so many composers who write their music in isolation and then don't receive the glorious opportunity to hear it played for months—even years! That's why I'll always stay on the road with my expensive gentlemen."

The next sentence was out of my mouth before I could stop it: "I don't think I'll ever be good enough to play in your band."

Duke fixed his eyes right into mine. "I've heard you play, Daniel. You're working hard and you're improving all the time. You couldn't find finer teachers than Rex and Cootie. But . . . playing in my band is like playing baseball for the Kansas City Monarchs—you have to be among the very best. Not only that, but I want musicians with their own individual sound. That's what I'm looking for—individuality. Believe it or not, when I write music I'm thinking of my individual musicians and what they bring to the table. So I'm not writing a part for trumpet—but for Cootie's trumpet. I'm not writing music for an alto saxophone—but for Rabbit's horn."

"Do you think I'll ever get my own individual sound?" I asked.

Duke looked out the window and then back at me. "Could be—I hear promise in you, lad. But it takes years of study and practice. However, in the meantime, I have an offer. I need someone to copy my music for me—for example, to copy the parts for the trombone players, and the part for the reeds. Interested?"

"But I can't read music," I said.

"I'm willing to teach you."

And that's how I became Duke Ellington's musical copyist, a job I held for many years. Although Duke would allow me to blow a blues or two when the hour was late and the crowd was thin, I simply never had the gift. What some supremely talented people don't realize is that it isn't all practice—it's a precious prize, from God or nature or luck. I don't know if Rex and Cootie ever realized what supreme artists they were. I hope they did. Now I'm not a *wretched* musician— let's not go there—but I simply did not possess the unique gift it took to play in Duke Ellington's Famous Orchestra.

The waiter returning, Duke paid the bill, leaving (as always) a generous tip. "Do you remember your parents at all?" he asked out of nowhere.

"No—I was just a baby when they died."

Duke was quiet for a moment, gazing out the window at the church across the narrow street. "My mother died four years ago and it almost did me in." He smiled. "But I saw the tough times through." He stood up. "Now, I'm going to go to the theater to become acquainted with its piano. Care to come along?"

"No thanks, Duke," I said. "I just want to wander around the city for a spell."

He squeezed my shoulder. "You're a good man, Daniel. I'm proud to know you. Our lessons begin tomorrow."

They did, too—and those lessons handed me a fine career.

Fourteen

After Brussels we played Antwerp, Belgium, then on to the Netherlands, where Duke and his band appeared in The Hague, Utrecht, and Amsterdam.

As our train sped across the thawing, springtime fields between the cities, we again saw men (and women) placing machine gun posts in ditches and haystacks.

"Gives me the willies," said Ivie, gazing out the window.

Around two o'clock in the morning on April 9, our train crossed the border between the Netherlands and Germany, but I was asleep and didn't notice. The plan was to scoot right through Nazi Germany on our way to our next show in Copenhagen, Denmark. I woke at dawn to a great deal of commotion and noise.

"What's wrong?" I asked.

"The train's been stopped in Hamburg, Germany," said Barney, looking pale. "The Nazis are checking our papers and not allowing us to leave."

My heart was suddenly throbbing in my throat. Quickly, I washed my face, brushed my teeth, dressed, and headed to the dining car. Breakfast was being served as always, but outside the windows was the shadowy darkness of the Hamburg station. Even Duke, who usually lounged about in his blue bathrobe until at least noon, was dressed in his crispest suit, speaking with a Nazi official. Swarms of the Nazi police called *Gestapo,* wearing gleaming black helmets and boots, had entered our train.

"You have no right to hold us here," I could hear Duke saying to the official, who then spoke in accented English about taxes that must be paid to the *Reich*—("That's the government," explained Rex).

After several minutes of wrangling, the official clicked his heels and stalked off the train, his Gestapo in tow. Duke managed a smile. "Well, folks, he says that we're here for at least six hours, so let's just relax and have our breakfast."

Yet no one (except Duke) was hungry. Digging into his usual mountain of food, he said, "There must be a fine blues tune lurking in this situation somewhere. The *Herr Hitler Blues*, perhaps."

"The *Evil Nazi Blues*," suggested Tricky Sam.

"I got it—The *Godforsaken Gestapo Blues*," said Rabbit.

Riding on Duke's Train

"The *Black Folks Stuck on a Train in Naziland Blues*," said Harry.

I wasn't much hungry and besides being quite frightened, I was bored. Hour after hour passed with no word from the Nazis. A few times the Gestapo outside would cup their hands around their faces and gaze in at us, as if we were circus animals or something. Steely-eyed, and their mouths were unsmiling slits.

"That's it, Nazi," said Ivie, "get a good look at the exotic black folks. Watch out, though—we bite!"

At one point I looked out the window and saw an elderly couple, dressed in black, trying to buy something from a food vendor. The old man was paying for his food when three Gestapo officers appeared. Descending on the couple like a pack of dogs, they kicked and shoved the old man and his wife away from the vendor's stand.

"Prejudice is lovely, isn't it?" said a voice behind me. It was Otto, looking both angry and disgusted. "Those old folks are Jewish—the same as Jesus."

"Why are those Nazis so filled with hate?" I asked.

"Good question, Daniel," replied Otto. "From what I've read, their leader, Adolf Hitler, has filled their heads with ridiculous notions that they're the *Master Race,* better than the rest."

"So that gives them the right to kick those old folks?"

"No, of course it doesn't," said Otto, "but they seem to think it does."

Close to noon, Rex crooked a finger to signal that I should follow him out of the dining car. In the baggage car, Harry and Cootie were waiting, looking like guilty schoolboys. "Hey, Dannyboy," said Harry, "we're busting out of here for a few hours. Want to come along?"

"But what if the train takes off without us?" I asked, picturing us stranded in the streets of Hamburg, Germany, surrounded by Gestapo, with no way out.

"No chance of that," said Rex. "The Gov'nor says that we won't be leaving anytime before dark. He knows we're going for a stroll and won't take off without us."

"But why do you want to leave the train?" I asked. It seemed to me that we were unlocking the cage and climbing in with the lions.

Cootie chuckled. "We're hungry—and we figure that a place named *Hamburg* must have mighty tasty hamburgers!"

I wasn't sure if he was kidding or not, but I found myself saying, "Okay, I'm with you."

My three friends pounded me on the back. "Good man, Dan!"

It was one of those grouchy gray days that seems to be always threatening rain, but remains dry. Several

Gestapo saw us leave the train, but for some reason said not a word. The neighborhood surrounding the train station was industrial, with roaring, smoke-belching factories.

"Where are all the people?" asked Cootie.

"They're inside those factories," replied Rex, "making bullets."

Soon, though, we turned a corner and found ourselves in a shopping district, bustling with streetcars and people, who sure seemed surprised to see three black men and a black boy in their midst. Some pointed, but all stared.

"I hope you guys are remembering the way back to the train," I said, "because I don't have a clue."

Harry tapped his temple. "Don't worry, it's all up here."

Rex pointed to his own behind. "This would be more accurate," he whispered with a wink.

"These folks are staring so much," said Cootie, "that I feel like I'm naked or something."

"There's no Harlem in Germany," said Rex. "They've probably only seen black folks in pictures."

"Yeah," said Harry, "like that one." He pointed to a wall filled with posters of various sizes and shapes. One, in sickening color, showed a grinning black musician gripping a saxophone. His lips were grotesquely fat, his nose flattened like a pancake, his white teeth grinning like a simpleton. *Verboten!* the poster read in fat black letters: *Niggermusik! Verboten!*

"What does *verboten* mean?" I stupidly asked.

"I'm not sure," replied Rex, "but I'm sure it's not *loved* or *respected.*"

Just then several things happened at once, none of them good. A whistle blew, then another, followed by another. Shouted voices called out to us in guttural squawks. We turned to see three Gestapo officers chasing after us, their pistols held aloft.

"Run!" screamed Cootie, grabbing me by the collar.

Fear filled every nook of my brain. *Nazis!* If it hadn't been for Cootie's strong right arm, I would have froze. As it was, my heart pumping like a train engine, I hightailed it with my friends around a corner. I figured that tall Harry and short Cootie would be swift, but I was surprised by how fast Rex's chubby little legs were carrying him. The adrenaline was flowing and I was soon having no trouble keeping up with my friends. I counted *one . . . two . . . three* pistol shots, hoping that they were aimed to the sky. The Gestapo's whistles seemed to pierce my eardrums.

"Down here!" yelled Harry, and we dashed around a corner into a narrow street, luckily empty of pedestrians. Leaning over, I almost vomited.

"Black men! Black men!" called a voice up ahead. At first I figured that one of the Gestapo had broken

away from the others, rounded the corner up ahead, and fooled us. *"Black men! Black men!"* But the voice belonged to a young man, dressed in a black turtleneck sweater, gesturing from a shop doorway. *"Here! Here!"* Hearing the Gestapo's whistles blowing feverishly nearby, having little choice, the four of us careened into the doorway.

"Quick! Quick!" hissed the young man.

His shop was filled with radios, records, and record players. Looking genuinely frightened, he rolled away a radio on wheels, lifted a square of red carpet, and opened a trap door built into the wooden floor. A wooden ladder trailed down to who knew where.

"Quick—down!" hissed the young man.

The Gestapo's whistles now sounded as if they were in the same street as the shop. Shrugging, Harry led the way down the ladder, the three of us close behind. *Slam!* the trap door was shut, leaving us in total darkness. I could hear the wheels of the radio being rolled back over the red carpet.

The ladder descended into darkness. Harry, reaching the bottom first, whispered, *"Be careful."* A few more steps and he had me by the waist, yanking me away from Rex and Cootie's feet. Soon the four of us, breathless, stood in the dark, hearing faint voices above speaking in German. Stupidly thinking that perhaps the Gestapo could hear my breathing, I held my breath for as long as I could—which wasn't long. I felt as though my heart would splatter out from my ribcage and land with a loud *sploink* on the floor, tipping off the Gestapo to our whereabouts.

A warm, strong hand gripped the back of my neck. "*Shhh* . . . just breathe in, breathe out, breathe in, breathe out. . . ."

Whatever the conversation was up above, it seemed to go on for hours. Suddenly—*bam!*—the lights were snapped on. We stood in a spacious basement, filled with leather couches, chairs, and a windup Victrola record player. The trap door in the ceiling opened and down scrambled our turtlenecked savior.

"They're gone," he panted, and it was clear from his face that he was as frightened as we were. Holding out a sweaty hand, he said in precise, heavily accented English, "My name is Klaus. I'm proud to call myself a Swing Kid as well as being the recording secretary of the Hamburg Hot Club."

Harry, shaking his hand, said, "Nice to meet you, Klaus. I'm—"

"No! I know who you are," said Klaus, his face beaming with pleasure. "You," he said, touching Harry on the shoulder, "are Harry Carney, the baritone saxophonist of the Duke Ellington Orchestra. You," he said, touching Rex, "are Rex Stewart, the cornettist in Duke's band, and you," he said, touching Cootie, "are Cootie Williams, the great trumpeter who took the place of the late, lamented Bubber Miley in 1929." He stood in front of me. "You, I'm not so sure of."

"I'm Danny," I said, shaking Klaus' hand. "I polish Sonny Greer's drums and try to avoid playing poker with Ivie Anderson."

"Ah, Ivie," said Klaus, "a true angel in song." Bowing to us, he seemed deeply touched. "I cannot tell you how much your music means to me and my friends and what an honor it is to meet you." Tears stood in his eyes; he brushed them away with the sleeve of his sweater. "But I forget myself. Can I offer you wine? Beer? Coffee?"

Rex, Cootie, and Harry all looked at each other, grinning. "The three of us will have beers," said Cootie, "and the young one will have a coffee."

"No, thanks," I said.

"I will be right back," said Klaus. "Please, sit down and make yourself at home. I just want to call several fellow members of the Hot Club. They will not believe me, but they will never forgive me if I fail to call. I told the Gestapo that I saw you running away and I have locked my shop, so that the danger is gone. I will return shortly, gentlemen."

In no time at all, Klaus and his three friends— two young men and one pretty girl, barely out of their teens—climbed down the ladder, each of the men carrying steins of frothy beer. Introductions were made—to tell you the truth, I've forgotten the names of the other three—and we all sat down on the couches to talk.

"But what are you doing in Hamburg?" asked the young girl. "We heard that the Nazis would not let you play here."

"That's right," said Rex, who winced at his first sip of German beer. ("It was as warm as rat piss," he told me later, "but we were too grateful to complain"). "However, we have to cut across your country to reach Denmark, and the Gestapo are holding up our train at the station."

Klaus' eyes were actually filled with tears. "The pigs! First they ban swing records and dancing, then they do not allow you to play your glorious music for us true believers, and now this."

"They're just playing with you, of course," said one young man, who was wearing a beret. "They wouldn't dare harm the great Duke Ellington."

"I hope you're right," said Cootie.

Cupping his chin in his hands, Klaus said, "Cootie, you made your first recording with Duke on March 7, 1929."

"Hmm, yes," said the other young man, who wore his bangs combed forward. "It was *The Dicty Glide*, recorded for Victor."

I thought that Cootie's eyes would bug out of their sockets. "Yeah, that's right, that's right. But how do you *know this*? I'd forgotten all about that record."

Leaping to his feet, Klaus opened the door of a closet, in which hundreds of records were carefully stacked. He quickly found the one he was looking for, placed it gingerly on the Victrola, gave it a wind-up, and in a few seconds the scratchy, exciting sounds of '29 vintage Ellington filled the basement. Since the four Germans sat back, closed their eyes, and listened, Rex, Cootie, and Harry did the same. ("Never close your eyes around strangers," Granny always warned me, and I heeded her advice). When the song had finished, Klaus wound up the machine for another play.

"I can hear you in the background on your beautiful baritone, Harry," said the beret fellow.

"Yup, that's me. We haven't played that tune in ages. Quite good, I must admit."

"Is that Freddy Jenkins or Artie Whetsel on the other trumpet?" asked the banged fellow.

"It's Artie," said Cootie. "Poor devil, he's been mighty sick."

"Ah," said the girl, "and there's Rabbit. Where's he right now?"

"On the train," said Rex, "probably grumbling."

Then commenced a questioning worthy of a fine detective: *What is Duke like?* (Tough question to answer, that). *What was it like to pal around with Bubber Miley?* (Big smiles with that one). *How much are you allowed to improvise on Duke's compositions?* (Depends—sometimes a great deal). *Who's playing clarinet on this record—is that Barney?* (No, it was Harry!) *What is going through your mind when you're on stage improvising, practicing your art? Rex, how is it different playing in Duke's band rather than Fletcher Henderson's?*

It was easy to see that my three friends were immensely flattered, quite amazed that foreigners knew their work so thoroughly. Then, however, it was *our* turn to throw out the questions.

"You said before, Klaus, that you're a Swing Kid," said Rex. "What *is* that?"

Klaus' upper lip was covered with beer foam. "It's a young person who lives and breathes for jazz or *swing music*. We consider the terms the same."

"So do we," said Harry.

Beret Fellow leaned forward intensely. "It means to worship the spirit of jazz that allows each musician to be *himself*—whether he is white Bix Beiderbecke, white and Jewish like Benny Goodman, or black like yourselves." He spat on the floor. "But the Nazis have hounded us and made our music—*your* music—illegal. They call it *degenerate*. It is they who are degenerates!"

"Of course Nazis are going to hate jazz," continued

Bang Fellow. "It represents *freedom*—the freedom of the musician to play his soul on his instrument. Only a degenerate could find fault with such a ravishing music." (Rex beamed at the compliment).

Cootie cleared his throat. "I hear you, man. But how are we going to get past these degenerates and back on our train?"

(*What's a degenerate?* I thought to myself. *Look it up next time you see a dictionary*).

Klaus smiled. "Oh, I have that all figured out, Cootie. Don't you worry. We have just one request first."

For a flash the musicians looked suspicious.

"Could you please autograph my book?" Klaus was holding a copy of a book I'd seen Rex reading: *Le Jazz Hot* by a Frenchman named Hugues Panassie. (I remembered seeing old Hugues talking to Duke backstage in Paris). Klaus' copy was battered and dog-eared.

"You got it, brother!" said Cootie. "Hand me a pen." And Harry, Rex, and Cootie wrote messages and signed their names in our new friend's book.

Beret Fellow, Bang Fellow, and the Pretty Girl scrambled about the basement, soon returning with three more copies of Panassie's book, which they all seemed to hold as some sort of musical bible. Duke's men dutifully wrote more—(I glanced over Rex's shoulder: *Keep the faith, brother/sister!* was his message)—

in each book and handed them back. The four young Germans now held their copies as if they were sacred.

"Now here's my plan," said Klaus. To me his plan sounded simple—but workable. After embracing all four of us—the *Fräulein* smelled quite tasty—Klaus and his friends climbed the ladder to see if the street outside was empty. It was, so Klaus drove the store's van to a back entrance. "I'm always delivering radios that I sell or fix," he explained. Luckily, the back of the van had no windows and the four of us squeezed in. Before slamming the back door, Beret Fellow said, "Klaus will drive as close to your train as possible. When he opens the back door, run like devils. Good luck and keep on swinging, cats!" We were left in darkness.

Soon the van was chugging along. Since we were bouncing around like ping pong balls in a hurricane, it was lucky that the station was not too far away. During the brief trip, however, we slammed off the van's metal walls and each other.

"My cousin Ray," said Cootie, "works in Mobile, Alabama loading and reloading ships all day. 'I'd give anything to live your life, Coots,' he always says to me. And you know, right now . . . I'd *still* rather be me!"

We all laughed, but not too loudly.

The van halted. We could hear Klaus fiddling with the back door lock. I'm sure that my friends' hearts were beating as wildly as mine. Suddenly we saw daylight, and heard Klaus' voice, "Go, my friends, go," and then we were running like madmen through the station's doors to our train which, thank God, was still there.

Although we received quite a few looks, we hopped back onboard the dining car before any of the Gestapo could react.

"And where have *you* been?" asked Ivie, in the midst of a poker game, her winnings spread out before her.

"*Went . . . looking . . . for . . . a . . . ham . . . bur . . . ger!*" panted Harry.

Ivie looked mad. "Well, did you bring the lady back a burger?" she demanded.

Unfluttering his handkerchief, Rex mopped his damp brow. "Sorry, Ives. I told and I *told* Danny not to scarf down that last burger—*Ivie's gonna want that one, boy*—but he wouldn't listen."

My Ivie only smiled at me. "That's alright, Danny. I started a new diet this morning anyway."

A sudden thought slapped my brain. "*Rex! The fortune teller!*" I cried.

Mopping his brow one last time, Rex folded up his handkerchief. "What are you talking about?"

"In Paris—that old lady fortune teller! *Do you like hamburgers?* she asked. You said, *Yes*, and she said . . . *Don't!*"

Chuckling, Rex said, "Well, I'll be skinned alive . . . don't that beat all. . . ." Whipping out his calf skin journal and licking a pencil, he began to write down his latest adventure as a member of Duke Ellington's Famous Orchestra.

• • • •

It was past midnight when the word arrived that we were free to leave the station and the country.

"Good riddance," said Rabbit under his breath as our train built up speed.

Around three in the morning, however, we were stopped again at Flensburg, near the German border with Denmark. "Nothing to worry about, folks," said Duke in his blue bathrobe. "They simply want to check our passports." Since Duke was the only one not grumbling, I figured that he'd been up composing his latest piece. The rest of us, though, had been woken out of our dreams.

"The Nazis are doing this just to hassle us," said Jimmy, who looked like a little boy in his light blue pajamas.

Three Nazi officers, dressed of course in black, stepped onto the train. It seemed that only one could speak English. "I'm very sorry to awaken you," he said, "but I have my orders. Your passports, please."

One by one we filed past the three, handing them our United States passports. The only one of us not in pajamas or a bathrobe was Ivie. Hurriedly, she had gotten dressed.

Now Sonny's real name was William, which was naturally what it read on his passport. The Nazi, glancing at the passport, said, "Hello, Sonny, how you doing?"

Sonny was in no mood for conversation. "My name's William."

The officer smiled. "Go ahead, your name's Sonny. I saw you in Chicago at the Oriental Theater in 1934!"

Turned out that this Gestapo officer was a huge Ellington fan who had asked for this duty. I heard him say quietly to Duke, "If it was anyone else, you'd be held up for days here at the border simply to frighten you. But all I'm going to do is check the passports and you'll be on your way."

"Much obliged," said Duke, but without his customary smile.

Within thirty minutes our train was chugging smoothly along and when we passed the border out of Nazi Germany and entered Denmark, I felt like a soul liberated from Hell who had just waltzed into Heaven.

"Don't worry, folks," said Duke before returning to his composing. "We'll be taking a boat out of Sweden when we leave for England. No more journeying through Germany."

And of course, in the years after 1945, when the world learned what the Nazis had done to the Jewish people in Germany and across Europe, I thought back to the elderly couple abused for simply trying to buy food in Hamburg—and of Henri, the generous Jewish gentleman in Paris. Did the Nazis leave Chanel and her family in peace? God, I hope so.

Thinking, too, of Klaus and his fellow Swing Kids, reminded me that not every German had been a Nazi.

Fifteen

The band's show the next evening in Copenhagen had an edge, to say the least. The way Ivie swung into *It Don't Mean a Thing* made the crowd as one leap to its feet and dance. Rex's performance on *Boy Meets Horn*, usually so sly, was tonight a declaration of pride, as if his cornet was telling the people, "I am *me!*"

"That was smoking," Rex said well after midnight, as we stood on the deck of a large ferry taking us across a narrow stretch of the Baltic Sea to Malmo, Sweden. Jonesy and I had worked like madmen to load up the ferry with our equipment, instruments and bags, for a new train awaited us in Sweden. "A show like that reminds me why I play jazz—because it's *different* every night. I can't imagine being a classical cornettist, playing the *same* music the *same* way every night. Man, if I'm angry or edgy or feeling a tad down, why, it all comes out in my horn." Rex gazed down at the frothy water. "That's why being a jazz musician is being an artist in the truest sense of the word, and *that's* why the Gov'nor is just as important a composer as Mozart or Bach. He's just writing his music for *today*."

"He *is* driven, isn't he," I said, huddling in my coat against the damp chill.

"Well, get this: Duke decided last week to give up drinking. Now, he was never a drunk, but he could hold his own. 'I'm retiring as the undefeated champion,' he said in that fancy way of his. I asked him why, and he said: 'Drinking wastes too much energy that I wish to put into my composing.' Now *that's* dedication."

"You talking about me again, Fat Stuff?" said a voice. A warm hand squeezed the back of my neck. It was Duke.

"You know it, Gov-nor."

"Have you completed your exercise yet, Daniel?" Duke asked. Good to his word, he had begun teaching me the rudiments of reading and copying music. To my surprise, I found it rather easy.

"Yup—in about twenty minutes before the show. I *think* it's right."

Another neck squeeze. "I'll look it over tomorrow after breakfast." Duke looked out over the dark water, pulling his coat tight around his neck. "We're a long way from True Reformers Hall, Fat Stuff. Remember those days?"

"'Deed I do," said Rex. "Old Room Ten, with that battered old piano and you trying to hypnotize the nearest pretty filly with that smile of yours."

"That smile has served me many a main course over the years. . . ."

Although I didn't get the joke, both Duke and Rex cracked up.

"I'll never forget old Doc Perry," said Duke. "Why, that man had the longest finger spread on the keyboard that I've ever seen. He was patient with the youngsters, too. Old Doc taught me a great deal."

"Maybe that's why you're always so patient with the young ones," said Rex.

Duke smiled. "Maybe. But I figure we're only here on this rock for our seventy-so years and we might as well be decent to one another."

I decided I'd remember Duke saying that—*We might as well be decent to one another*—and try to keep it as my pocket philosophy.

"You know," continued Duke, "I've read the critics who call me a genius, and, yes, that certainly can brighten up one's day. But if certain people hadn't *encouraged* me and *helped* me when I was younger, would I have had the confidence to write the music I've written—or would I have just given up?" We left that question unanswered. "Look! See that light up ahead, fellas?" We did—small and indistinct, but there. "That's Sweden." *Time to load up the band's stuff onto yet another train, I thought.* "Oh, and Daniel, now that you're my copyist, you can retire from your career as an exquisite lugger. I wired ahead for some workmen to schlep our equipment onto the train." He smiled that smile. *Hypnotic*, Rex called it. *Mysterious*, I called it. "But as a personal favor to me, please keep on polishing Sonny's drums. I don't know what the old dog would do without you."

"Sure, Duke."

Another neck squeeze, and he was gone.

Sixteen

Early on the morning of April 29, 1939, I awoke in our hotel room in Stockholm, Sweden to the sound of a jazz band.

Rex opened one eye. "That doesn't sound like Tricky playing records. That sounds live."

Someone was knocking on our door. It was Rabbit. "This is beyond crazy," he said. "You have to see this."

More craziness? The night before, as our train zipped from Jonkoping to Stockholm, every train platform in every town and village had been filled with folks, many holding torches, waiting to catch a glimpse of Duke. As the train would slow down (but not stop) at each platform, we could hear the voices in the crowd, many singing Duke's songs in Swedish accents.

Down the hall Duke's door was open wide. Unlike us, the Gov'nor enjoyed a suite and inside a sixteen piece (I counted) jazz band was playing a tune to Duke, who was seated on the couch in his blue bathrobe, beaming like a little boy, surrounded by a bursting garden of flowers.

"It's the Swedish version of *Happy Birthday*," he shouted over the rather strident band. "They certainly blow with gusto!"

Seeing the perplexed look on my face, Rex leaned down and whispered, "Today's Duke's fortieth birthday. This is nuts!"

"Happy birthday, Duke!" I yelled over the band.

"Thank you, lad!" he shouted back. "May your fortieth be as sweet!"

Downstairs in the hotel's restaurant the celebration continued as we chowed down breakfast. Even Duke, who usually kept his cool, always in command, seemed genuinely touched by the Swedish people's generosity and love.

"Pass the word, Daniel," he whispered to me. "Band rehearsal at two this afternoon right here in the hotel's ballroom." After spreading the command, I just wanted to be alone for a spell. All of the noise and commotion had me a bit exhausted. Grabbing my bag of dirty clothes, I wandered the streets surrounding the hotel until I found a laundry. I left it off with a smiling old woman who spoke no English except, "One hour done, one hour done."

Soon I found myself on a bench beside Stockholm's harbor, watching the boats bounce up and down with the current. Nearby bobbed a house boat. A little girl was hanging her family's wash on a clothesline strung across the deck. Catching sight of me, she kept looking and then looking away. *No big deal*, I thought to myself, *she's just never seen a black person before.* (The evening before, Tricky Sam had watched the people greeting us at the train station and said, "Bet you any amount, Dannyboy, that the only black folks in Sweden right this minute are in the Duke Ellington Orchestra!") Still, it was strange how this girl, who was blonde and about my age, kept stealing looks at me. Then I about fell over when I heard her call in a thick Southern accent: "Mama, there's a colored boy out here!"

Both of her parents appeared on deck. "Are you from Africa?" called the father.

"No, Georgia," I said.

"A fellow countryman!" bellowed the father, a slender gent. "Come on aboard!"

Figuring that with a little girl around I was in no danger, I scampered onboard the house boat and shook hands all around. The father was George, the mother Margaret, and the girl Susan. The smells of coffee and bacon were rising up from below decks.

"We're about to eat," said Margaret, "and there's plenty of food if you'd like to join us."

Too polite to say that I'd already had breakfast (and too hungry already), I joined them at a small table on deck.

"So what is a Georgia boy doing here in Stockholm?" asked George, who seemed a friendly sort. (Back home in Georgia, to tell you the truth, Granny and I had had little to do with white folks).

I explained.

"Back when we were courting," said Margaret, "we'd listen to Duke's band from the Cotton Club on the radio. Remember, George?"

He did. Now I asked, "And what are *you* folks doing here?"

Turns out that they were poor Texas farmers who had hit oil on their land and were poor Texas farmers no longer. "We've been living on house boats for the past two years all across Europe," said Margaret. "Not the same one, of course. We lived in a house boat on the Seine River in Paris, on the Thames in London."

"We lived in Amsterdam for a while," said Susan.

"And now we're here in Sweden," said Margaret. "Lovely people."

"But we're thinking of going back soon," said George. "There's a war coming and we don't want to be stranded here in Europe. When are you folks headed back?"

"In about a week," I said. "Duke says that we're

sailing to England to see if we can play a few shows there. Then we're heading home on a boat called the *Ile de France*."

"Heard of it," said George. "Perhaps we ought to think of booking passage, dear," he said to his wife.

Margaret smiled. "It's just been lovely escaping the Texas heat for a spell."

We then talked about the sights we'd seen and they agreed that Paris was something special. We talked about home and the South. Granny had never trusted white people, and had trained me to avoid them, but these folks were friendly and the color of my skin didn't seem to matter a whit to them.

"Duke's playing tonight at eight at the . . . hold on a second." I pulled a piece of paper out of my pocket. "The place is called the *Konserthuset*," I said, "and I can tell Jonesy—that's Duke's valet—to leave three tickets for you if you'd like."

George looked at Margaret. "What do you say, Darlin'? Want to cut a rug tonight?"

It seemed to me that Margaret blushed. "Oh . . . *you*," she said, as Susan rolled her eyes. (Even though I missed old Granny, the thought of being stuck with her on a house boat for any spell of time gave me the shivers).

We said our goodbyes and much to my surprise I was able to find my way back to our hotel.

Seventeen

"Alright, gentlemen," called Duke from his piano bench. "I'm calling it *Serenade to Sweden*. I wrote it last night and I'd like for us to play it tonight."

We were in the hotel's ballroom and none of Duke's musicians seemed happy to be there.

"Two o'clock in the afternoon," grumbled Otto. "Man, Duke, it's time for my afternoon *nap.*"

Duke, dressed down in gray slacks and an old gray sweater, smiled his far-off smile. "You can sleep when you're dead, Otto. That's my plan, anyway. Plenty of time for snoozing when I'm gone."

Standing at the hotel's piano, Duke tickled a few notes. "Although Daniel here has been learning quite quickly how to notate my music—and we'll be using his talents in the future—there was no time to write this all down, so we're going to learn it together. Rex, you're first."

Rising from his chair, his trusty cornet by his side, Rex said, "Ready, Gov'nor." Duke played eight notes at the piano over and over—each note rising higher than its previous neighbor, but in an amiable, un-rushed manner. Listening with his eyes closed, Rex smiled. "That's quite tasty," he said.

"Ready for a helping, Fat Stuff?" asked Duke from his piano bench.

"Ready." Bringing his horn to his lips, Rex played Duke's eight notes with precision and soul.

"Okay, Tricky, your turn," said Duke, waving his arms over his head.

Closing his bulging eyes, Tricky Sam waved his rubber plunger across the bell of his trombone, produc-ing his sly, conversational *wah-wah/yah-yah* sounds— yet the beauty of Duke's melody still shone through.

"Over to Harry."

Lifting his baritone sax, Harry played Duke's new tune with his customary skill and deep-in-the-belly beauty. Sitting down, he shot me a wink.

"Now the entire band," said Duke—and darned if they didn't all blend their sounds beautifully around the tune, harmonies and all. I can't explain why, but I could feel tears coming to my eyes. The band's sound was just so . . . *perfect*.

"That was great, fellas," said Duke. "Cootie—now give it some Mobile tang."

My friend poured some Alabama hot sauce all over the melody and, with Duke's swinging arms leading the way, the band brought it all home.

Serenade to Sweden. Duke and his men recorded it in June after we returned home from Europe. Listen to it sometime.

• • • •

That evening's concert at Stockholm's *Konserthuset* was one of the finest performances I ever saw Duke and his men give. Before they even played a note, ten little girls in white dresses strolled shyly onto the stage to present Duke with ten bouquets of flowers and sing *Happy Birthday* in accented English.

Standing next to me off stage, Ivie whispered, "You know, this show is being broadcast all over Sweden. The whole nation is listening to us!"

"Thank you, young ladies," said Duke into his microphone. "You bring a touch of class and dignity to our rather rag-tag collection of musical *mysteriosos.*"

"What the heck is he *on* about?" whispered Ivie. "And who's he calling *rag-tag*?"

Duke was still talking: "You have been so overwhelmingly lovely to us that we have cooked up a new number just for you, tonight. Ladies and gentlemen: *Serenade to Sweden!*"

It was amazing to hear the song that I heard taking shape only hours before played so perfectly—as if the band were playing *The Mooche* or *Stompy Jones*, songs they had known for years. I could only see the folks in the first few rows, but many of them had tears in their eyes, too.

If I live to be one hundred—which I just might—I'll never forget the sight of Ivie, gorgeous in her white gown, singing the Swedish national anthem. She sang the song phonetically—yet still sounded as if she meant every word. "How's *that* for *rag-tag*?" she snapped at Duke as she breezed past his piano bench.

Several hours later, after playing the sixth encore, with the crowd still wanting more, Duke said, "Sweden treats artists with such respect and indulgence. *Please always know that we love Sweden madly! Good night!*"

By midnight we were on a boat for England. Duke's room was next to mine and I fell asleep to the sound of a piano. The man was writing yet another tune.

Duke Ellington created music the way other folks create breath.

He couldn't stop.

Eighteen

A huge full moon hung over London.

"Do you think it's open?" asked Rabbit, holding his precious alto saxophone.

"The only way to know is to try the door," said Rex, bounding up the steps of Westminster Abbey.

This was our second day in the ancient city. Duke had been scrambling with music union officials to see if the band could play a show or two in England, but so far he'd been shut down. (Somehow I couldn't picture *any* person—official or not—not caving in to Duke and his charm). As soon as we had landed at the Savoy Hotel, Sonny had doffed a bowler hat and disappeared with Harry. "They've probably sampled the beer in every pub in town by now," said Rex with a grin. Ivie, dressed to the nines, had waltzed through the hotel lobby.

"Wither are you going, Madame?" Rex asked.

"I'm going to get my hair done in the finest salon on the Strand," she replied, gliding out through the hotel's revolving doors like the Queen herself.

And we—Rabbit, Rex, and I—were now trying the doors of Westminster Abbey which, to our surprise, opened right up.

"Tallyho, it's dark in there, gents," said Rabbit in his best British accent. "Watch your step."

The smells of burning candles and incense greeted our noses. Moonlight was spilling in through stained glass windows, leaving a trail of rainbow light across the stone floor.

"Just think," said Rex. "Kings were being coronated in here nine hundred years ago! Shakespeare probably walked down this very aisle."

"I want to stand in front of the altar," said Rabbit.

In a few seconds there we were, standing before the golden and silver altar, with not a soul about.

Finding a seat and kneeling down, I said a prayer for Granny while watching Rabbit fiddle with his mouth piece, which he always kept in his pocket. Once it was attached to his saxophone, he raised his horn to his lips, closed his eyes, and blew the saddest, most achingly lonely melody. Listening, I was reminded of nights lying in bed, hearing the winter winds whip around our cottage. I was reminded of how I feel when I realize, with sudden clarity, that I will not always be alive. The tune reminded me of the ache I still feel when I realize how I was cheated out of having a mother and a father.

Rabbit's melody was that sad—and that beautiful.

As the last note faded to the ornate ceiling high above, Rabbit lowered his sax and smiled. "Duke and I cooked that baby up back in March. I'm for calling it *Night Wind*, but Duke's calling it *Finesse*. Maybe we'll compromise."

"Hey, scoot over, Daniel," said Rex. In a moment the three of us were kneeling before the altar, listening to the silence.

There's a famous photograph, taken during the Nazi Blitz of London, that shows Westminster Abbey surrounded by explosions. Night after night—from September, 1940 to May, 1941—the Germans flew over and bombed London and other British cities, killing over 40,000 souls. Yet Westminster Abbey, along with St. Paul's Cathedral up the road, survived. When I see that photograph, I think back to this night in April, 1939, and how peaceful the church, and all of London, seemed.

Rabbit, though, disturbed the peace with a gentle karate chop to the back of my neck. "You've got it made, kid," he said.

"What do you mean?"

"I heard Duke talking to Ivie about how quickly

you're catching on to copying music. You have a job for *life* if you want one, my friend."

"Really?"

"You bet." Rabbit smiled his cynical smile. "Duke doesn't pay much—but he pays on time."

Rex snorted. "Don't listen to him, Daniel. Rabbit makes more than any musician in Count Basie's band. He's not starving."

Rabbit pulled his hat down over his eyes—always a sign that the argument was over. "Yeah, well, he could be paying me more. That's all I'm saying."

Soon we were walking along the darkly moving Thames River, with Big Ben still lit up. It was one minute to midnight. "Just watch," said Rabbit. I did—nothing happened. "Keep watching." At the stroke of midnight the lights switched off and Big Ben, too, was dark.

Rex yawned. "Let's hightail it back to the hotel. Tricky said that Ivie (with her new fancy hairdo) was going to organize a huge poker game—and I'm feeling lucky tonight."

Nineteen

Two mornings later our latest ship, the *Ile de France*, stood ready to depart from Southampton, England. Duke, Ivie, and I stood at the railing, surrounded by hundreds of other passengers. Duke's normal cool was not in evidence. "Where in the devil can they *be*?" he growled.

The ship, having already given three massive groans from its horns, was ready to depart—but neither Sonny nor Tricky Sam was on board.

"Were they at your infernal poker game?" Duke asked Ivie.

"Hey, now lay off my poker game. Many are the men who can buy their wives some goodies with the loot they win at my games. I'm helping the economy, Duke. President Roosevelt would be proud."

Despite himself, Duke couldn't help smiling. "And what becomes of the loot *you* win, my dear?"

Ivie's lovely eyes scanned the docks, which were filled with folks, many of them crying. "Every penny goes to my poor, widowed mother, Duke—you know that."

No one paid any attention to us. The passengers crammed against the railings were waving to their friends and relatives on the docks. Ladies waved handkerchiefs, men waved hats, and many eyes were wet with tears. (I often wonder if any of these dear people waving their goodbyes were later killed by Nazi bombs). Everyone seemed to know that war was up ahead—the biggest war this world has ever seen—and that the people sailing for America might never see their loved ones again.

After a blast from the ship's horns that you could feel in your chest, the gangplank was yanked on board and the *Ile de France*, pulled by three tugs, inched out of Southampton's harbor. Seagulls whirled overhead.

"Well, that's it," said Duke. "I'll have to do the explaining to their wives. Sonny's wife already hates me."

"*Duke—look!*" yelled Ivie.

A small yellow dinghy, with an oarsman and two passengers, had taken off from a beach to the left of the docks. Two men in brown suits and brown bowler hats stood in the bow, waving to us. One of the men turned, seemingly encouraging the oarsman to row harder.

"It's Tricky and Sonny!" cried Ivie.

Looking about frantically, Duke spied a crew member. Dashing over, he grabbed the man by the arm. "Could you tell the captain to please slow down the tugs? We have two more passengers to take on board." The crew member saluted the Duke and took off.

Within ten minutes, both Sonny and Tricky were climbing a rope ladder onto the deck of the *Ile de France*. "Tell the Queen that I won't be over to the palace tonight for tea, dear chap," Sonny called down (in an upper crust accent) to his oarsman, who doffed his cap in reply.

"How in the world?" asked Ivie, punching Sonny (hard) in the chest.

Tricky, his sleepy eyes even sleepier, folded his arms protectively across *his* chest and said, "We emptied our pockets of two nights of poker winnings, that's how."

"The chap drove a hard bargain, too," said Sonny, smiling like a sweepstakes winner, still talking in his hoity-toity accent (which he wouldn't abandon until we were halfway across the Atlantic).

Duke, rolling his eyes, headed below decks to his cabin, most likely to write some music (just for a change).

I'll never forget standing at the railing, watching

England recede into the distance. It was May 3, 1939. On September 1, all of Europe would be thrown into war. Duke would not return to Europe until 1948.

• • • •

This crossing was nothing like the journey over. The ship was packed to the gills and several storms had folks ralphing up each and every meal. (I scoured the ship for them, but I never saw George and Margaret and Susan, the good folks from Texas). I don't recall a day when the sky wasn't iron gray and the sea roiling with white caps. One morning after breakfast, wishing to escape the sights and sounds of green-faced folks, I stood at the railing, watching our ship plow through the angry Atlantic.

"Sure smells down there," said a voice. It was Juan, the quiet trombonist. Along with Harry, he was always the first on stage before a show, carefully preparing his instrument for the music ahead.

"I guess I'm lucky," I said. "Sea sickness just doesn't affect me."

Juan looked out to sea. "Me neither." We were quiet for several minutes before he spoke again: "You're lucky for another reason, too."

"What's that?"

"Duke likes you. You seem to be catching on with copying his music—a job, I might add, he used to have *me* do."

I thought of the knife that Juan was supposed to carry. "I'm sorry. . . ."

He smiled. "No, no—I'm glad not to do it anymore. Gives me more time to practice my horn. The trombone is an unforgiving instrument. If you skip just one day of practice, you certainly can feel it the next. But what I mean is that you could have a job for life here, if you want it."

"But why wouldn't I want it?"

Throughout our conversation, Juan didn't once look at me. "Oh, it's fine as long as you're single. But once you find the right girl, settle down, and have a son or daughter, it eats away at you. My wife and kids—two of them, a little boy and a girl—see me for a few days every two or three months. My daughter's only three and she cries when I pick her up. It's like I'm a stranger."

"I'm sorry," I said. I'd mistaken Juan's silences and grim looks for anger. Maybe he simply lived in a state of constantly missing his loved ones. I wondered how many of Duke's other musicians felt the same but were better able to hide their aches.

He patted me on the back. "Not your fault, kid," he said, walking off.

• • • •

A week after we'd left Southampton, the *Ile de France* slowly glided into New York Harbor on a drizzly, foggy evening, the lights of Manhattan all ghostly and damp. It was May 10, 1939. I stood at the railing with Barney, Rabbit, and Harry as we passed the Statue of Liberty.

"Man," said Barney, "I've never been so glad to see that stern old gal!"

As the ship eased into its berth on the Hudson River, Duke's band—wiped out, unshaven, green around the gills—staggered down the gangplank.

"Will you look at old Ivie," said Rex. "Out of all of us, she's the only one who looks presentable."

"That's because out of all of us," said Ivie, "I'm the only one who believes in regular bathing."

In the fog it was difficult to see below us, but a sudden roar exploded as an invisible crowd spotted Duke and his musicians. Then the cheers and whistles grew louder and louder. As we touched land, folks lifted Duke, Harry, Rabbit, Rex, Jimmy and the rest of the band onto their shoulders and paraded them past the docks to the street. Two men tried to lift Ivie, but she slapped their hands away, smoothed out her skirt, and walked like royalty to a taxi.

Jonesy looked as tired and hangdog as anyone I'd ever seen. "Ready, Danny?" he asked me. "Let's get to work."

"What do you mean?" I asked.

"Didn't Duke tell you? The party's over. We're back

to unloading the suitcases and instruments. He said that he'll call for a truck to arrive here as soon as he gets back to Harlem. We'll load up the truck and then our work will be done."

At three in the morning, when my head finally hit the pillow in my bedroom up in Sugar Hill, I was asleep in a second—and I slept until nine o'clock the next evening. But the last thing I heard before I fell asleep and the first thing I heard when I awoke was the sound of Duke at his piano, composing music.

We were home.

Twenty

But not for long.

Within a week we were once again on the road. Climbing aboard Duke's silver train in Penn Station, my heart broke as I saw Juan saying goodbye to his wife and children. All four of them were crying.

This tour swung across the country—Philadelphia, Pittsburgh, Columbus, Akron, Cleveland, Toledo, Detroit, South Bend, Chicago, Milwaukee, Omaha, Lincoln, Wichita, Denver, Salt Lake City, Reno—before landing in California, where we spent a week in San Francisco and a week in Los Angeles.

Then we swung back across the country, this time taking the southern route: San Diego, Phoenix, Albuquerque, Amarillo, Oklahoma City, Tulsa, Little Rock, Memphis, Nashville, Knoxville, Charlotte, Virginia Beach, Richmond, Washington, Baltimore, Philadelphia, and home once again to New York.

This was my life for the next thirty-four years. By the 1960s we traveled to Europe—now by plane—as often as we had once traveled by train to Fargo, North Dakota. The Middle East and India in 1963. South America in 1968. Japan, Hong Kong, Australia and New Zealand in 1970, the year Rabbit died. The Soviet Union in 1971. Ethiopia and Zambia in 1973. In October of 1973 Duke premiered his *Third Sacred Concert* in London's Westminster Abbey. Naturally, I was responsible for writing down the score for each musician, and when I was finally finished with my work, near two o'clock in the morning, I took a solitary stroll through the ancient church.

As my feet echoed on the stone floor and I breathed in the scent of incense and candles, my thoughts traveled back to that long ago night in 1939 when I'd walked the same aisles with Rabbit and Rex. Both of my friends were now dead, with only Harry and Cootie left from the old days.

Old Rabbit died in his dentist's chair. Despite their arguments over loot, Duke was shattered.

My dear friend Rex died in 1967. His wonderful book, *Jazz Masters of the 30s*, scribbled in his calf-skin journal, written with love and soul, was published five years later.

I was the one who found Tricky Sam asleep forever in a San Francisco hotel room in 1946. Beside him on the bed was a book by his man, Marcus Garvey—and his trombone.

Poor Jimmy, always wracked with a cough, only made it to the age of twenty-three. Tuberculosis ran him down in 1942.

And my dear Ivie, the big sis I never had, died in 1949 from emphysema. She was only forty-four.

I was now a forty-six-year-old man who, following Juan's advice, had never married.

My heart nearly stopped when a voice called out, "Who goes there?" Peering through the gloom, I saw that it was Duke, wrapped in a long black coat.

"What are you doing here, boss?" I asked, knowing that he hated to be called that.

He wrapped an arm around me. Though still possessing his disarming, sarcastic smile, Duke was now an old man, with massive bags beneath his eyes. "I could ask you the same, Daniel."

"I love London," I said. "I was thinking of being here with Rex and Rabbit in '39. One night we snuck into this very church and Rabbit blew a version of *Night Wind* that was beyond beautiful."

He smiled. "Rab could do that, couldn't he? You know, I tell the reporters and the biographers that I don't look back, but that's not exactly true. I'm forever getting down on my knees to pray for the folks I miss."

We were silent for several moments. "I think I miss

Ivie the most," I said.

Duke sighed. For once, I felt that his mask was down. "She loved you so much, Daniel. You know, I should have married that girl. I was simply too stupid to appreciate her."

His arm was still on my shoulder. Looking into his tired eyes, a sudden thought hit me: *This man is the closest you've ever come to having a father.*

Turning, Duke began to stroll toward the altar. A slight movement of his hand let me know that I was to follow.

"You know, lad, I'm not going to be around forever."

"Don't talk that way, Duke."

"Oh, stop it. You have eyes—you can see it's true. When I'm gone, I've left you a tidy sum of money in my will. I want you to buy a home for yourself, find a good woman, and settle down. You don't want to be an old cat like me—still dragging his tired behind from joint to joint."

I couldn't stop the tears. "Hey, but look around— not a bad joint to be playing in."

Stopping, Duke slowly surveyed Westminster Abbey from corner to corner. "Ah, but you should've seen the Cotton Club in '27. Now *that* joint was swinging. Beats the pants off this place."

• • • •

The concert next day was, of course, a triumph. As

the audience brought Duke back for an encore, old Harry shot me a wink from behind his baritone saxophone. From my customary spot on the side of the stage, I knew what dear Harry's wink meant:

We've all enjoyed quite a life, haven't we?

Within a year, both Duke and Harry were gone, and my career with the Duke Ellington Orchestra was over.

Only hours before he died at New York's Columbia Presbyterian Hospital, Duke requested that an electric keyboard be placed across his lap.

Composing—creating—right up to the end.

That was Duke Ellington.

Epilogue

Duke, of course, was good to his word. I haven't had to work a day since.

Yes, good reader, I was once as young and speedy as you. However, I am now an old man, with a balding dome and a creak in my stride.

Don't laugh. With a bit of luck, it will happen to you, too.

In 1948 Duke's orchestra had played a series of engagements in Dublin, Ireland. Before continuing on into Europe, we'd had a few rare days off. I'd rented a car and taken off with Rabbit into the green heart of the Irish countryside, and that's when I discovered Avoca, the most beautiful village in the world.

Duke's funeral was held on May 27, 1974, at the Cathedral of St. John the Divine. More than ten thousand people packed the church, while at least two thousand more paid their respects outside.

The next day I packed my clothes and few belongings and by nightfall was eating my dinner in Fitzgerald's Tavern, shocked to discover that Avoca had not changed a whit in the previous twenty-six years. Old gents in corduroy (several of whom were later to become dear friends) were seated at the bar watching a football match on the television. As I sat alone at a table in the corner, I attracted some not unfriendly curiosity, for it's not often that a black man comes to town.

After dinner, the sky was an orangey Celtic twilight as I took a stroll. Main Street was empty, the shops closed, with the road running up a hill. At the crest stood a solid stone church, St. Mary & Patrick—built by local miners in 1862, a plaque told me. Standing at the crest of the hill, I turned and gazed open-mouthed at this lovely village.

To my left, the church, and indeed the entire village, was dwarfed by a timber-carpeted hill that rose up behind it. All of Avoca is watched over by this hill; before a rainstorm the scurrying clouds seem to rise from within it. The only sound was the cooing of birds that the locals later told me were doves. Several homes were lit up behind their curtained windows. Taking a deep breath, I tried to imagine living here, with a protective hill behind my home. Bordering the village on the right is the Avoca River, which runs beneath an ancient stone bridge. Everything was so quiet that it seemed strange to remember my Harlem apartment (where I'd awoken only twenty hours earlier) with its constant screams of sirens and horns.

The very next day a realtor showed me my snug white cottage built on the hill that overlooks the village and I've lived here ever since. Two years later I met my Elizabeth and in short time we had our daughters, Hannah and Sarah, who are now grown and married.

From Georgia to Manhattan to Ireland. It's been quite a life.

Now that we're older, my wife likes to sleep late. However, I've always been an early riser and I'm usually up and about by five. After a mug of tea, I take my morning walk to the Meeting of the Waters, a beautiful spot where two rivers, the Avonbeg and the Avonmore, merge. A leafy park juts out to the spot where the two rivers converge. It was at this very place that Thomas Moore wrote his famous poem *Meeting of the Waters*:

> *There is not in this wide world a valley so sweet,*
> *As that vale in whose bosom the bright waters meet.*
> *Oh! the last rays of feeling and life must depart,*
> *Ere the bloom of that valley shall fade from my heart.*
>
> *Sweet Vale of Avoca! how calm could I rest,*

Riding on Duke's Train

In thy bosom of shade, with the friends I love best.
When the storms that we feel in this cold world should
cease,
And our hearts, like thy waters, be mingled in peace.

Here I sit most mornings, an old, old man, alone and thinking, surrounded by the gentle sounds of the waters, the birds, and the breeze.

In the distance are green hills and on the crest of one is a lone white cross. It reminds me of Granny and of her Pentecostal church back in Georgia. I sit there and pray for all of the people I've known who are no longer, realizing that one day *I* will be no longer.

If there *is* a Heaven filled with all of my old friends—Duke, Ivie, Rex, Jimmy, Harry, Cootie, Rabbit, Tricky Sam, my parents and Granny—then I'm all for going there. Count me in. But if there is not, if it's only a tale, then my soul will be quite content, thank you, to laze and listen to the blending rivers at the Meeting of the Waters. I guess I'll find out soon enough.

A lovely inn and pub overlooks the spot and on Sundays, weather permitting, there are open air concerts of Irish music. Although I was never quite good enough to play trumpet in Duke's band, I've kept my lip strong with practice and I enjoy playing. "Now don't overwhelm us, Dan," says Daniel Cahill, the

159

leader of the band. "My poor tin whistle doesn't stand a chance against your blasts." So I try to blow mellow and pretty, just like Rex did, and mingle in with the music like the two rivers below us.

Tourists, naturally, are always about and many times I fall into conversation with New Yorkers who fill me in on the city and all its doings. No one, though, has ever hailed from Sugar Hill and I wonder if it's still as leafy and quiet and majestic as it was when I lived there with Duke and his family.

And all of this—my wife, my daughters, my home, my strolls, my Sunday afternoon tootings, my Irish life—I owe to Duke.

• • • •

Nailed into our living room wall is a rough wooden bookcase, filled with hundreds and hundreds of compact discs, which I began to collect as soon as they existed. With a few exceptions—Louis Armstrong, Billie Holiday, Ella Fitzgerald, Charlie Parker, Don Byas, Lester Young, Coleman Hawkins—most of the discs contain the music of Edward Kennedy "Duke" Ellington, my friend and employer. From 1926 to 1973, he recorded hundreds and hundreds of times, either in the studio or in concert.

Duke wrote several thousand compositions, all of them enriching, exciting, beautiful. "I am trying to express American music as I hear it and know it," he once said. From lush popular songs to pounding dance numbers, from swinging ballets to "tone parallel" symphonies, from "musical portraits" to jackhammer blues, Duke Ellington wrote it all. He is America's Beethoven, America's Bach.

Or, perhaps, those two esteemed gentlemen are Europe's Duke Ellington.

Right now the sun is going down over our hill and I want to hear some Duke music. Here we go: *Serenade to Sweden*, written to honor the people who made his fortieth birthday so special. I remember. I was there.

Duke Ellington's music will always exist for you to explore, to enjoy, to dance to. It's like a precious gift just waiting to be unearthed. Duke's music will enrich your life. I promise.

• • • •

What are you waiting for?

Duke Ellington Time Line

1899: Edward Kennedy Ellington born in Washington, D.C. on April 29.

Circa 1914: Duke composes first tune, "Soda Fountain Rag."

1916: Duke plays professionally for first time; he wins, but turns down, scholarship to study art at Pratt Institute.

1923: With Sonny Greer and Otto Hardwick, Duke ventures to New York City. He returns home to Washington, yet returns to New York again, this time to stay.

1926-1927: Duke writes (with Bubber Miley) and records his first masterpieces, "Black and Tan Fantasy" and "East St. Louis Toodle-Oo." Harry Carney joins band; he will remain until 1974. Joe "Tricky Sam" Nanton joins band; he will remain until his death in 1946.

1927: With his ten piece band, Duke opens at Harlem's Cotton Club on December 4

1928: Johnny Hodges joins band.

1929: Cootie Williams joins band. He will leave in 1940 and return in 1962.

Timeline

1931: Duke releases his first extended composition, *Creole Rhapsody.*

1933: Duke Ellington and his Famous Orchestra tour Europe for the first time to wide acclaim.

1935: Duke's mother dies. In grief, he writes *Reminiscing in Tempo*, his longest work yet.

1938: In Pittsburgh Duke meets 23 year old composer Billy Strayhorn. This gifted composer, arranger, and pianist will be with Duke for 28 years.

1939: Strayhorn, bassist Jimmie Blanton, and tenor saxophonist Ben Webster join band. In spring, Duke's orchestra tours Europe for the second time; they are briefly detained in Nazi Germany.

1941: Duke's innovative musical, *Jump For Joy*, runs for 11 weeks and 101 performances in Los Angeles.

1942: Blanton dies on July 30, only 23 years old.

1943: On January 23, Duke premieres his "Tone Parallel to the History of the Negro in America," *Black, Brown & Beige*, at Carnegie Hall.

1945: Ellington's band is chosen to play music on the air on the day of President Roosevelt's death.

1946: Duke premieres *The Deep South Suite.*

1947: Duke premieres *The Clothed Woman*; *The Air Conditioned Jungle;* and *The Liberian Suite.*

Timeline

1950: His first long-playing (LP) album, *Master-pieces by Ellington,* is released. Duke writes his fourteen minute suite, *Harlem.*

1951: Johnny Hodges, Sonny Greer, and Lawrence Brown leave Duke.

1956: Johnny Hodges returns to the fold; Ellington stages a remarkable comeback at July's Newport Jazz Festival, with tenor saxophonist Paul Gonsalves' 27 chorus solo setting the night on fire. The resulting live album becomes Duke's all-time best seller and he is featured on the cover of *Time* magazine.

1956-57: Ellington & Billy Strayhorn premiere *A Drum Is A Woman* and *Such Sweet Thunder.*

1959: Duke writes *The Queen's Suite* for Queen Elizabeth II and composes the soundtrack to the film, *Anatomy of a Murder.*

1960: Ellington & Strayhorn compose the soundtrack to the film, *Paris Blues,* as well as the suite, *Sweet Thursday.*

1963: The Ellington Orchestra tours India and the Middle East. Duke and Strayhorn write *The Far East Suite.* Duke composes *My People* for Chicago's Century of Negro Progress Exposition.

1965: Duke composes his *Concert of Sacred Music,* later performing it in cathedrals around the globe.

Timeline

1967: Billy Strayhorn dies. The Ellington Orchestra records ...*And His Mother Called Him Bill.*

1968: Duke premieres his *Second Sacred Concert.* The band tours Mexico and South America.

1969: Duke celebrates his 70th birthday at the White House; President Nixon awards him the Presidential Medal of Freedom, our nation's highest civilian honor.

1970: Johnny Hodges dies. Duke releases *New Orleans Suite,* containing Johnny's last recordings.

1971: Duke and the Orchestra tour the Soviet Union and Europe.

1972: Duke and the Orchestra tour Hong Kong, Taiwan, the Philippines, Japan, Burma, India, Singapore, Ceylon, Malaysia, Indonesia, Australia, and New Zealand.

1973: Now ill with cancer, Duke premieres his *Third Sacred Concert* at London's Westminster Abbey.

1974: Mid-May: Duke sends out his Christmas cards early. While hospitalized for cancer, he continues to work on *Queenie Pie* and *The Three Black Kings.* Duke Ellington dies at 3:10 a.m. on May 24, 1974. Over 10,000 mourners attend his funeral in Manhattan's Cathedral of St. John the Divine, while over 2,500 stand outside.

The Musicians Riding on Duke's Train

Edward Kennedy "Duke" Ellington (1899-1974)

Jazz music's finest composer, Duke was the leader of his own orchestra from 1926-1974. A tireless composer, Ellington wrote over 2,000 pieces of music.

Johnny "Rabbit" Hodges (1907-1970)

A poet on his instrument, Hodges is one of jazz's finest alto saxophonists.

Harry Carney (1910-1974)

Duke's trusty baritone saxophonist stayed with him from 1927 to 1974. Ellington's closest friend in the band, Harry died only five months after Duke.

Joe "Tricky Sam" Nanton (1904-1946)

Tricky Sam was a master of muted, conversational trombone playing as well as the art of the poker face.

Ivie Anderson (1905-1949)

Ivie was the greatest singer that Duke Ellington ever hired. In my opinion, she's in the pantheon with Billie Holiday, Ella Fitzgerald, and Sarah Vaughan.

Jimmy Blanton (1918-1942)

Blanton, the great revolutionary of the jazz bass, was dead before his 24th birthday. He brought startling melodic conception to his rhythmic instrument.

Sonny Greer (1895-1982)

One of Duke's oldest friends, Sonny was the band's drummer for close to thirty years.

Django Reinhardt (1910-1953)

Django was jazz's first great non-American musician. His guitar playing, in tandem with Stephane Grappelli's violin, is still enjoyed world over.

Barney Bigard (1906-1980)

A great New Orleans clarinetist, Barney later played with Louis Armstrong's All-Stars.

Rex Stewart (1907-1967)

Rex Stewart was not only a supreme artist on his cornet: His superb book, *Jazz Masters of the Thirties*, should be required reading for all jazz fans.

Juan Tizol (1900-1984)

Duke's valve trombonist, because of his light complexion, often darkened his face when the band played the

American South. Tizol also co-wrote with Ellington great tunes such as "Caravan."

Lawrence Brown (1907-1988)

Brown's mellifluous trombone first graced the band of Louis Armstrong, before "The Deacon" joined the Ellington Orchestra for two stretches: 1932-1951 and 1960-1970.

Otto Hardwick (1904-1970)

Along with Sonny Greer, Otto was one of Duke's oldest friends in the orchestra.

Cootie Williams (1911-1985)

Bubber Miley, who died young in 1932, was Duke's first great trumpeter; Cootie was his second. Jazz fans wept when Cootie left the Duke in 1940, but he returned in 1962, remaining until after Duke's death .

Songs Mentioned in "Riding on Duke's Train"

Page 16: "Mean Old Bedbug Blues" (Wood) recorded by Bessie Smith 1927
"West End Blues" (King Oliver) recorded by Louis Armstrong 1928
"Solitude" (Ellington) recorded by Duke Ellington and His Famous Orchestra 1934

Page 31: "Rockin' in Rhythm" (Ellington & Carney) recorded by Duke Ellington and His Famous Orchestra 1931

Page 32: "Rose of the Rio Grande" (Warren/Forman/Leslie) recorded by Duke Ellington and His Famous Orchestra 1938
"Stormy Weather" (H. Arlen/T. Koehler) recorded by Duke Ellington and His Famous Orchestra 1940

Page 51: "Echoes of Harlem" (Ellington) recorded by Duke Ellington and His Famous Orchestra 1938

Page 53: "Jeep's Blues" (Ellington & Hodges) recorded by Johnny Hodges 1938

Page 59: "Boy Meets Horn" (Ellington) recorded by Duke Ellington and His Famous Orchestra 1938

Songs

Page 61: "Concerto for Cootie" (Ellington) recorded by Duke Ellington and His Famous Orchestra 1940

Page 77: "It Don't Mean a Thing (If It Ain't Got That Swing)" (Ellington) recorded by Duke Ellington and His Famous Orchestra 1932

Page 86: "Black and Tan Fantasy" (Ellington/Miley) recorded by Duke Ellington and His Famous Orchestra 1927

"Prelude to a Kiss" (Ellington) recorded by Duke Ellington and His Famous Orchestra 1938

"Mood Indigo" (Ellington) recorded by Duke Ellington and His Famous Orchestra 1930

"Old King Dooji" (Ellington) recorded by Duke Ellington and His Famous Orchestra 1938

"Blue Ramble" (Ellington) recorded by Duke Ellington and His Famous Orchestra 1938

"Dusk in the Desert" (Ellington) recorded by Duke Ellington and His Famous Orchestra 1937

Page 91: "Montmartre (Django's Jump)" (Rex Stewart) recorded by Rex Stewart and Django Reinhardt 1939

Songs

Page 93: "Braggin' in Brass" (Ellington) recorded by Duke Ellington and His Famous Orchestra 1938

Page 116: "The Dicty Glide" (Ellington) recorded by Duke Ellington and His Famous Orchestra 1929

Page 134: "Serenade to Sweden" (Ellington) recorded by Duke Ellington and His Famous Orchestra 1939

Page 140: "Finesse (Night Wind)" (Ellington/Taylor) recorded by Duke Ellington, Billy Taylor, and Johnny Hodges 1939

The Author

Portrait by Hannah Carlon

Mick Carlon is well into his third decade as a public school English teacher at both the high school and middle school levels. When not grading papers, he can be found driving his wife, Lisa, and daughters, Hannah and Sarah, crazy with his incessant playing of jazz CDs. "Jazz musicians are among America's most fearless artists, and if young people will only give the music of artists such as Duke Ellington a try, they will make an enriching friend for life." Carlon's novel on Louis Armstrong, *Little Fred and Louis*, will be published by Leapfrog Press in 2013.

About the Type

This book was set in Adobe Caslon, a typeface originally released by William Caslon in 1722. His types became popular throughout Europe and the American colonies, and printer Benjamin Franklin used hardly any other typeface. The first printings of the American Declaration of Independence and the Constitution were set in Caslon. For her Caslon revival for Adobe, designer Carol Twombly studied specimen pages printed by William Caslon between 1734 and 1770.

Designed by John Taylor-Convery
Composed at JTC Imagineering, Santa Maria, CA